WINTER OF GRACE

ROBERT FUNDERBURK

BETHANY HOUSE PUBLISHERS
MINNEAPOLIS, MINNESOTA 55438

Winter of Grace
Copyright © 1998
Robert W. Funderburk

Cover design by Eric Walljasper

Published by Bethany House Publishers
A Ministry of Bethany Fellowship International
11300 Hampshire Avenue South
Minneapolis, Minnesota 55438
www.bethanyhouse.com

Printed in the United States of America by
Bethany Press International, Minneapolis, Minnesota 55438

Library of Congress Cataloging-in-Publication Data

CIP data applied for

ISBN 1–55661–616–3   CIP

To
Lucille and Jann,
who "oft refreshed me."

And to
Ashley Landry,
our "second daughter."

CONTENTS

PROLOGUE

"Please don't make that awful noise again!" the little girl whispered to herself. "And don't hurt anyone this time."

Named Laura Lee after her mother, she had celebrated her seventh birthday the previous month—if you could call sharing a pack of week-old cinnamon rolls in a pickup camper with her father and his seventeen-year-old brother, Caleb, a celebration. Her blond hair, once golden but now dulled by oil and dirt, hung in stringy disarray about her thin shoulders. Eyes as blue as periwinkle in sunshine carried a slight glaze as though shielding her mind from the things that a child shouldn't have to see.

From the cab of the battered Chevrolet pickup, Laura gazed at the Fire Chief gasoline pump in front of the grocery store. Blood Hound, Brown Mule, and Canonball chewing tobacco signs decorated the store's paintless board wall. Among the signs, a hand-lettered square of cardboard warned No Drinking Aloud.

Shivering in the chill dampness, Laura smelled the smoke of a coal fire rising from the chimney of the store, then shifted her eyes toward a huge maple tree, flaming with October orange, next to a barbwire fence.

Suddenly the roar of a shotgun and the sharp crack of automatic rifle fire from inside the store caused Laura to flinch. Slapping her palms against her ears, she watched the two men stumble backward through the door, the battered screen banging against the wall, then race for the truck. Their clothes splotched with black, green, and brown looked like pieces of the forest sewn into trousers and jackets. Bandannas covered their faces like those of the outlaws she had seen in the old westerns on their black-and-white television.

"Get this thang rollin'!" she heard her father call out as he jerked the door open and clambered onto the seat, dropping a brown paper bag on the floorboard. He gripped his AK–47 with both hands as he grimaced toward the dark interior of the little store.

Caleb stuck his .45 automatic inside his belt, leaped behind the wheel, and gunned the engine to life. "We almost bought it that time, Jack!"

"Not we . . . me," Ryder grunted through clenched teeth to the sound of gravel spanging off the truck frame.

For the first time Laura noticed the rip in the shoulder of her father's jacket . . . and the dark, damp stain spreading in the heavy cloth. She forced herself to look away.

"Maybe we'd better get you to a doc." Caleb gripped the steering wheel with both hands, his eyes fixed on the road that twisted along the valley floor.

"You know we can't do that. Gunshot wounds gotta be reported to the police." Jack propped his weapon against the seat, reaching into one of the deep pockets of his jacket. Taking out a soiled green handkerchief, he folded it twice, shoved it beneath the jacket, and pressed it against his shoulder with the flat of his hand. "Besides, that ol' geezer jes' ripped a little hunk of meat loose. It'll be all right soon as the bleedin' stops."

Laura stared through the rain-streaked windshield at the smoky mist rising from the folds of the tree-covered mountains as though coming from fires banked deep inside the earth. With the pickup spinning along through the wet Appalachian gloom, she watched the massive walls of black shale hanging above them on either side like portents of a dark winter ahead.

Laura stared at the tombstones in the old cemetery behind the little white church gleaming dully in the afternoon mist, its steeple rising toward a lead-colored sky. Most of the stone markers were weathered and mossy and tilted with age, but her grandma Ryder's new tombstone stood straight and shiny beneath the deep red leaves of a single dogwood tree.

She remembered walking the autumn woods the year before with her grandmother as she told stories of her family who had lived in the Smokies for two hundred years. Since her grandmother's death, Laura's world had grown more and more silent. She felt that her words were no longer important to anyone.

"We gotta leave these mountains, Caleb." Jack Ryder squatted on his haunches among the graves.

Laura stood next to Minnie Ryder's grave, thinking of the sugar cookies she had baked last Christmas. She could almost smell the rich fragrance in the kitchen and remembered the delight of seeing the little snowmen and reindeer as her grandmother lifted them out of the oven. She always got the first one out of the pan and could almost taste that first warm, soft, sweet, delicious bite. The conversation between the two men had become little more than a drone that only occasionally forced its way into the quiet memories that were becoming more real to her than life.

"Yeah. That ol' man in the grocery store was ready for us with his shotgun. He dropped it in a hurry when you cut loose with that AK–47, though." Unconsciously his hand brushed against the handle of the automatic stuck in his belt. "Word's out now. Next time we might not be so lucky."

"I don't think they've put any names to us yet, but somebody's bound to recognize our camper sooner or later."

"Where you wanna go?"

In her dreamworld, Laura Lee sat in her grandmother's lap, watching the yellow flames and red coals in the fireplace, listening to that soft voice and the words of the old, old story of Jesus blessing the little children.

11

Her father got to his feet, rubbing his palms together briskly. "Someplace warm." He glanced at the tops of the pines swaying in the wind. "I ain't looking forward to spending another winter in these mountains."

"Jack . . ."

"What?"

"Maybe we could just get jobs." Caleb gave his brother an oblique glance. "You know . . . when we get to someplace else."

"You already forgot how long I tried to get work?" Ryder's dark brown eyes took on a strange and violent light. "Come home from Nam and get spit on and called 'baby killer.' Then the only job I can get is a stock clerk at the Jitney Jungle or driving a bread truck." He picked up a dead limb from the ground and flung it into the woods. "Then Wanda up and leaves me flat. Woman never was no good anyhow."

At the sound of her mother's name, Laura felt herself drawn away from her memories. She recalled the shouting and the crying and the tears running down her mother's bruised face—a face that was now blurred and indistinct, an image fading more and more with the passing of time.

Caleb gazed at Laura, still standing in front of his mother's grave. "I heard it all before, Jack. You always leave out the drinking and the drugs and missing work half the time when you *had* good jobs."

"Don't you smart mouth me, boy!" Ryder stomped over in front of his brother. "You hear me?"

At five eleven, Caleb stood three inches taller than his older brother, whose feats on the football field and prowess in barroom brawls had given way to a thickening around his waistline, the once-bulging muscles going soft. "I hear you, Jack."

"Just don't forget," Ryder growled, "I'm the only family you got left—like it or not."

"I know, Jack." Caleb returned his gaze to Laura Lee, dressed in a threadbare coat and dime store sneakers with no socks. "She hardly talks anymore, Jack. We need to find her a better place to live."

Ryder glanced at his daughter. "Her own mama didn't even want her. Who you think's gonna take her in now?"

Laura pulled her memories back around her, wrapping herself in their warmth. She saw again her grandmother's smiling face, her merry eyes twinkling in the firelight . . . and the voices of the men and the chill wind and the misty gray afternoon soon vanished as she sang along with her grandmother.

"Jesus loves me, this I know. . . ."

PART ONE

TOILS AND SNARES

1

WOMEN AND THE RIVER

"I'm so fat! I feel like a big-bellied rhinoceros."

Dylan opened the door of the blue Volkswagen bug and helped Susan out onto the grassy levee. Then he grabbed the picnic basket and the quilt. "All rhinoceroses are . . . is that right? Maybe it's rhinosceri."

Susan leaned into the slope of the levee and plodded upward. "Does it really matter?"

"Nah. Not unless you're a rhinoceros. You sure you're up to this picnic?"

Susan nodded in reply. "I want to do something besides sit around the house and visit the doctor's office. A little sunshine might be just what I need."

"Anyway," Dylan continued, "all rhinos are big bellied. Besides, you only weigh a hundred and thirty pounds."

Gaining the top of the levee, they started down toward the muddy, mile-wide river.

"But I'm only five three."

"You're eight months pregnant."

Susan breathed deeply as she took slow, deliberate steps, holding on to Dylan's arm. "I'm just ready to have this baby and start looking human again."

"You look absolutely beautiful."

Susan gave him a weary smile.

17

Dylan pushed a limb aside and guided Susan toward the end of the walkway leading out over the yellowish brown surface of the Mississippi River. A thick stand of willows concealed the secret place of Dylan's childhood on the river's west bank north of the Jackson Street Ferry and across from New Orleans. Over the years the boards had weathered to shades of gray and charcoal and brown. In some places, nails and bolts had given way, leaving gaps in the wharf's planking.

"So this is where you used to bring your old girlfriends." Susan St. John, her clear green eyes lighted with mischief, spread the handmade quilt on the weathered deck of the old abandoned wharf.

"They weren't so old." Wearing a white T-shirt with *LSU Tennis* lettered in purple and faded Levi's that were soft from countless washings, Dylan grinned at his wife, sat down, and leaned back against a wooden piling.

"You know what I mean."

"I only brought one out here, though. Her name was Becky, and we were about fifteen at the time."

"You're about to be a father," Susan said, sitting down and opening the picnic basket. "You shouldn't even *remember* the names of your old flames."

Dylan looked at Susan's dark, shoulder-length hair shining in the warm October sunlight, ruffling softly in the breeze off the river. "They all pale in comparison to you, sweetheart."

"I'll bet you say that to all your pregnant wives." Susan lifted freshly baked French bread out of the basket, pulled it from its paper sleeve, and began slicing it lengthwise.

"Only the ones that fix me oyster and shrimp po'boys." Gazing at the swell of his wife's belly beneath the lavender cotton dress printed with tiny white flowers, Dylan smiled with pleasure at the thought of becoming a father. In the autumn of the past year he had felt that his life was sliding inexorably into oblivion. Now he could find no words to express the gratitude he felt that he and Susan were still together.

"Well, why don't you help *this* wife get lunch on the table?"

18

She took two cold bottles of Barq's Root Beer beaded with drops of moisture out of a paper bag. "I forgot the opener. See if you can find something to open these."

Dylan took one of the root beers and placed the rim of the metal cap at an angle against the sharp edge of one of the dock railings, then thumped the top of the bottle downward with the heel of his hand, popping the cap off. "Here you are." Placing it on the planking next to Susan, he popped the other cap off and sat on the quilt while Susan prepared their lunch.

Susan's oval-shaped face, with its finely drawn features and skin as smooth and pale as porcelain, never failed to bring a pang of pleasure to Dylan's chest. He gazed at the single scar—a tiny white crescent at the left corner of her mouth. It gave her a vulnerable quality that made him feel that she was never quite safe when he wasn't with her.

Happiness had come to Dylan and Susan St. John's marriage in spite of the turmoil of their early years. Dylan thought of the trifling and selfish and uncaring way he had treated Susan back then and was grateful she had stuck by him. He realized better than anyone, after his carelessness had almost caused her death at the hands of an assassin's bullet intended for him, that the world would be a lonely and unforgiving place without Susan. She had been spared, and now he had determined to be the husband she deserved and soon the best father that he could be.

"Here you go, sport." Susan handed him a po'boy, heavy with fried shrimp and oysters and dressed with mayonnaise, lettuce, and sliced tomatoes.

Dylan held the po'boy carefully with both hands and took a big bite. Chewing with relish, he smiled his pleasure at his wife. "Mmm . . . that's good stuff."

"Don't talk with your mouth full."

Dylan nodded and swallowed. "Glad we came?"

"I am," Susan replied, gazing out over the sunlit surface of the water toward the great iron arc of the bridge and the towering buildings of downtown New Orleans beyond. "I truly am." She brushed her hair away from her eyes with the back of her hand. "I always enjoy spending time with your mother. I wish she had come with us."

"I think she wanted us to have this time to ourselves."

"I do, too, now that you mention it," Susan said and nodded. "You spent so much time away from home on that last case, I almost forgot what you looked like."

Dylan thought back on the weary nights as well as the hassle of New Orleans politics that had in some ways been worse than the actual tracking down of the assassin of several South Louisiana mayors. "I thought moving to Evangeline as Emile's chief deputy would get me away from all that political claptrap, but it sure didn't take long for it to catch up with me."

"This is South Louisiana, sugar. Politics, pralines, Mardi Gras, Tabasco, Cajun, and redneck . . . They all make one big Louisiana gumbo." Susan grinned. "If you left out one of the ingredients, the flavor just wouldn't be the same."

"I guess you're right. And maybe Evangeline is about as good a place as we're gonna find to live."

"I think so."

"And you don't miss the big city?"

Susan stared out across the river at the city of her birth. "I like to visit, but I don't think I could live here anymore. 'You can't go home again.' "

"Sounds like a good title for a book."

"I'm sure Thomas Wolfe thought so." Susan crossed her legs, leaning toward her husband. "You think you'll ever find time for your writing again?"

"Maybe . . . someday." Dylan glanced about the rickety old wharf. "It was right here that I first got interested in poetry."

Susan's eyes brightened with interest. "No kidding. You never told me that before."

"Becky read a poem to me." Dylan blurted the words out without thinking, then tried to make amends. "But that was a long time ago. . . . We were just kids."

"Tell me about it."

Surprised, Dylan looked at his wife's eager expression. "You really mean it, don't you?"

"Sure. I'm interested in everything about you. Especially something this important."

"But it happened with somebody else."

"Like you said, it was a long time ago and you were both just kids."

Dylan frowned. "You don't have to be so understanding, you know. You could be a little bit jealous."

Susan's laughter was as soft as the breeze though the willows. "Tell me the story, Dylan."

Dylan gazed down at the muddy, swirling currents that often made him think of the death of his father, Noah St. John, who had lost his life directly across the river at the Robin Street Wharf in his job as "walkin' foreman" with the longshoremen. "I think I remember that day so well because what happened seemed to help me get over losing Daddy."

"Tell me the story, Dylan," Susan repeated.

Dylan called back those Saturday mornings when his father had taken him to work, imagining himself perched high on a stack of wooden crates or on bales of cotton while his father moved among his men, overseeing the loading and unloading of ships. Those days seemed to belong to another life, during the times when he would escape the world in his refuge on the river that he had shared with only one other person.

"Dylan . . . are you all right?"

"Yeah." And that long-ago autumn day became real again as he told her the story.

It was a Saturday afternoon in early October, a little more than a year after Noah St. John had fallen between the dock and the side of a freighter, his body never recovered. The morning had dawned cool and crisp, but then the wind had shifted and cloud cover had moved slowly in from the south-

21

west like a gray blanket being pulled across the blue dome of the sky.

"Is the roast beef po'boy all right?" Becky Burke, her long blond hair perfectly straight, sat on a bench constructed of a rough two-by-twelve nailed between supports for the rusted ocher-colored tin roof. Her eyes were big and dark and somehow out of place in her bright face. She wore jeans, a navy sweat shirt, and the placid expression of a cloistered nun.

It could have tasted like ground glass and motor oil, and Dylan's answer would have been the same. "This is really great. Best I ever tasted." Wearing a *Holy Name Tennis* shirt and a pair of his father's old khakis, tattered and three sizes too big, he sprawled on a quilt his mother had made when he was a toddler. He smiled as he took another bite of the po'boy.

"I just love this place, Dylan. It's like nothing can touch us here." At fifteen, Becky shared the tenth grade as well as a love of the river with Dylan.

Chewing a mouthful of roast beef, French bread, gravy, and tomatoes, Dylan nodded his agreement.

Becky gazed out across the river toward the towering International Trade Mart building that stood at the foot of Canal Street. Beyond it the twin spires of the St. Louis Cathedral, oldest in the country, rose from the heart of the French Quarter. "Thousands and thousands of people all around us and nobody knows where we are. It's just perfect."

Dylan had been watching a curtain of rain that appeared upriver, reaching the mouth of the Harvey Canal and now was sweeping down the river toward them. Soon the first heavy drops dented the river's yellow-brown surface from shore to shore, and then it was upon them, pounding the tin roof like dull shrapnel. "Well, maybe not quite perfect."

A cold spray came blowing in, stinging their faces. Dylan grabbed the quilt and took Becky's hand, pulling her over to the lee corner of the open-sided shed. They sat on the floor, the quilt wrapped around them. He felt her hair, soft and fragrant against his cheek, as they watched the storm churn the river, turning the world a watery gray.

"This is even better than sunshine," Becky said, shivering slightly. "I just love the rain and the sound it makes on that tin roof."

Dylan stared out over the windswept water toward the Robin Street Wharf, a blurry outline in the heavy rain. He remembered huddling there beneath a makeshift shelter with his father in another storm. They drank coffee from a red Thermos and talked of going hunting together in the fall. He could see again his father's hard, callused hands, realizing for the first time how they revealed the character of the man. They were strong and dependable yet capable of great tenderness.

"You still miss your father very much, don't you, Dylan?"

Turning his gaze toward the willows bending in the wind, Dylan said, "I try not to think about it," his words almost lost in the storm.

"Sometimes I worry about you."

"Why?"

Becky pulled an emerald green scarf from her pocket, tying it around her hair that had been whipping about her face in the wind. "You seem . . . angry so much of the time. And it happens over things that shouldn't really matter."

"I don't know what you mean." Dylan shrugged.

"Like last spring when you got suspended two days for fighting," Becky sighed.

"He said my daddy was nothing but a dumb dock worker. You think I should have let him get away with that?"

"That's just ol' Freddy Hillman, Dylan. Nobody pays any attention to what he says. You know that."

"Yeah," Dylan agreed with a nod, "guess I just had a bad day or something."

Becky took Dylan's hand, squeezing it gently. "I don't want you to get expelled or anything. It might mess up your chances for a scholarship in tennis."

"I'll do better. Don't worry." Dylan felt the warmth of Becky's hand; could see another kind of warmth in her eyes.

"Playing tennis is the only way I'll ever make it to college. I don't want to lose out on that."

"It was a really dumb thing to do."

"What?"

"Freddy outweighs you by forty pounds. How could you think you'd win a fight with him?"

Dylan rubbed the side of his jaw, remembering the shock and pain of Freddy's big fist slamming into it. "That's just it. I didn't think." He grinned sheepishly at her. "You're right. It was a dumb thing to do."

Becky lifted her hand, touching Dylan on the side of his face with her fingertips. "You know I've known you for more than a year now. I'll never forget that day we met. It was September, the second week of school, in the hall after morning chapel. That was the same day your father got—"

"Yeah," Dylan interrupted her, not wanting the conversation to head in that direction, "and I swept you off your feet with my 'apple fritters' line."

"Well," Becky said as she compressed her lips, trying to suppress a laugh, "at least I could tell you weren't one of those smooth talkers who lie to girls about almost everything."

"It was all I could think of to say," Dylan admitted, "how much I liked apple fritters."

Becky squeezed Dylan's hand, then released it. She fished into her pocket and brought out a folded sheet of notebook paper. Opening it, she said, "I'd like to read something to you. I found it just the other day."

"I hope it's *Peter Cottontail*," Dylan deadpanned. "Read the part when he hides in the watering can from Farmer McGregor. That's my favorite."

Making a face at him, Becky cleared her throat. Her voice was soft and clear against the sound of the wind and the rain. "It's a poem called 'Adam's Curse,' and it's about a man and a woman who've been together for a long time. It takes place on a summer eve at twilight with the moon coming up."

"Whew!" Dylan blew out his breath. "That's a real mouthful for a little girl like you."

"I've not even finished my introduction yet," Becky said with a frown. "Anything worth having takes a lot of work. That's what the poem is really about."

Dylan adjusted the quilt over Becky's shoulder. "I'm not sure I can handle all this culture, Becky. After all, I'm the son of a dumb dock worker."

Becky gave Dylan a level stare. "You're not as dumb as you want people to think you are, Dylan St. John. Besides, you've got the name of a great poet." She smoothed wrinkles out of her paper and began to read, pronouncing each word distinctly and with the same inflection that her mother had used when she had read the poem to Becky the night before.

Dylan sat on the old dock at the southern end of the great river, a cold spray blowing across his face, and listened to the words of the Irish poet, born the same year the Civil War ended. Maybe it was Dylan's feeling for the girl and the sweet sound of her voice; the tragedy and loneliness that had come into his life with the loss of his father; the need for something to temper the awful reality of death. But the poet's words touched a part of him he never knew existed. It seemed as though he could almost feel a gentle hand caressing his soul.

Taking a deep breath, Becky read the last line, the sound of her voice dying away in the wind. " '. . . and yet we'd grown as weary-hearted as that hollow moon.' "

Dylan stared into her brown eyes, too dark for her fair skin and wheat-colored hair. He had no words to match the poem's unexpected effect on him. "That's nice."

"Nice!" Becky gazed out into the storm. "It's . . . it's just so beautiful." She placed her hand on the side of Dylan's face. "Dylan, I'll love you forever."

Somehow, even at fifteen, Dylan knew that forevers seldom lasted very long. Unable to repeat her words, he leaned forward and kissed her on the lips.

They sat together, quiet after the poem and Becky's words

of love, and watched the rain on the water until the first glimmering of blue appeared beyond the long curve of the river. The sun had broken through and touched the willows. They were bending over the water's edge, their long, dripping leaves shot with silver, like women come down to the river to wash their hair.

"That's a lovely story, Dylan."

Dylan pulled himself back from the past. The memory of that day had been so real he could almost feel the cold spray of rain on his face, although the sky was blue and mild above the tin roof of the old wharf. "And you're not even a little jealous?"

"Nope," Susan replied with a satisfied smile.

"Why not?"

She leaned over and kissed her husband softly on the lips. "Because I know how very much you love me."

The cemetery looked especially stark and lonely beneath the gray October sky. Its tombs stood in orderly rows like bulky white sentinels perpetually ready to escort any coffined guest across the portals of eternity.

Along one side, backed up against a piked iron fence, the "ovens" formed a high stone wall, sectioned off into neat rectangles, bearing a marked resemblance to oven doors, each holding one coffin. After a proper amount of time, the remains, coffin and all, were simply pushed into a small abyss at the back, readying the site for another occupant. They had lain fallow for years because the purveyors in the marketplace of death refused to make coffins small enough to fit the "ovens."

Dylan, wearing brown loafers, chinos, and a light blue button-down shirt, stood behind his mother as she fitted a bouquet of blue and yellow wild flowers into the slim concrete vase built into his father's tomb.

As he stared at the grave site, Dylan thought of the recurring dream that occasionally haunted his nights even fifteen years after his father had disappeared beneath the bluish oil-coated sheen on the brown water. There was always the siren call from the river, like a sweet and deadly voice that wanted to draw him through the willows onto the wharf, whispering, "Dive, dive into me, into the bright, soft flow of me, and swim forever with your father."

Helen St. John stood up, gazing down at the splash of color against gray weathered concrete. A light raincoat covered her charcoal skirt and white blouse. "I think they look nice, don't you? Noah always loved the autumn wild flowers. He said they were a sign that life still goes on, even when it seems like everything around you is dying."

"That doesn't sound like Daddy." Dylan sometimes felt that he had grown to truly know his father only since his death. He often wished he had taken the time to find out more about him while he was still alive. "It's almost like poetry."

Helen knelt and straightened a flower that had angled away from the others. "That's how I always felt about the letters he sent me when he was overseas. He could describe all the houses and smells and sounds . . . and people so well. It made me feel like I was right there with him."

Glancing to his left, Dylan saw a woman who looked to be in her seventies standing before one of the especially ornate "houses of the dead." Wearing a long black coat and a black lace mantilla draped over her hair and shoulders, she placed a bouquet of roses on a narrow shelf, then sat down on the edge of a marble slab and bowed her head. He got the impression that this was something, a ritual perhaps, she'd been doing for a long, long time.

"I'm so excited about the baby, Dylan." Helen sat down on an iron and wood bench that had been placed next to the aisle running between the tombs.

Dylan felt the damp wind stirring at the back of his neck. It brought a slight chill in spite of the muggy day. "I hope I can be as good a daddy as your husband was."

"You'll do just fine," Helen insisted. "And I couldn't have chosen a better mother for your child than Susan."

Dylan nodded his agreement. "Right now she's just ready to get the whole thing over with."

"I know exactly what she's going through. I felt the same way right before you were born." Helen brushed her hair back from her neck and clasped her hands together in her lap. "Is Susan all right now . . . I mean after her injury? She's not having any medical problems, is she? No trouble with the baby or anything?"

Dylan felt a stab of guilt as his mother asked about Susan's *injury*. "No. Everything's fine, Mama." He glanced at the woman in the black mantilla, her head still bowed as she slipped the beads of a rosary through her gnarled fingers, her lips moving in silent prayer. "Well, the doctor thought we probably should have waited awhile longer for her to get pregnant, until she got her strength back. But I guess there's no use going into that."

"Now, you can just quit blaming yourself for anything that happened, Mr. Dylan St. John," Helen said abruptly, her eyes sparking. "Susan and I have talked this all over, and we've decided that you can just take your load of guilt and dump it off the Mississippi River Bridge."

"Maybe I'll just do that," Dylan said with a nod. "But it still bothers me that—"

"That's enough!" Then the sparks in Helen's eyes died as quickly as they had flared up. "You've done some childish things in your life—like most men do, Dylan—but I can already see that you're becoming the same kind of man your father was. So you just forget about the past and let me enjoy being a grandmother." She held out a hand to her son.

Dylan took his mother's hand.

Helen gazed directly into Dylan's eyes. "Your daddy would be so proud of you now, son. I just wish he could be here with me to see his first grandchild."

"So do I, Mama."

Helen stood up. "We'd better be going. It's almost time to take your bride back to that pretty little cabin on the bayou." A sudden recollection lighted her eyes. "That reminds me. I ran into an old friend of yours who's moving out into the bayou country."

"Yeah, who's that?"

"Father Nick. You remember him, don't you?"

Dylan saw once more the short, slender priest who had taught him to play tennis for their high school team. "How could I forget him? I never could have gone to college without that tennis scholarship. Where's he going?"

"They're transferring him to St. Martin Parish. He said he's looking forward to a little peace and quiet after all these years in the big city."

Dylan smiled at the fond remembrance of the only man who had taken a real interest in him after his father's death. "Bayou Teche. It's pretty over there. Maybe I'll go see him sometime."

"I'm sure he'd enjoy that."

They left the cemetery and walked slowly past antebellum- and Victorian-style houses with second-story galleries, white latticework, and long porches with Greek columns. The old iron fences in front were never quite plumb and seemed to imitate the sidewalks that were tilted at odd angles by the tangled roots of the live oaks.

For as long as he could remember, Dylan had always liked to stroll along these sidewalks, old and broken and lovely, still holding to their purpose.

2

GONE SOUTH

Laura Lee stared at the tattered hole in her sneaker right next to Big Bird's yellow beak. She had loved the shoes since her grandmother had given them to her for a birthday present and was sad that they were wearing out, even if they did pinch her toes a little.

"Here you go, runt. Eat up."

Laura looked up from her seat on a stone bench on the lawn in front of the Evangeline Parish courthouse. Her uncle Caleb held out a paper plate of steaming food.

"It's crawfish stew." Caleb, in jeans and a blue cotton shirt, grinned down at his niece. "We're in Cajun country now. Might as well try some of this Cajun cookin' long as we're here."

Taking the plate and a tall bottle of Barq's Strawberry Soda, Laura Lee stared at the strange-looking concoction served on a pile of rice.

Caleb sat down next to her and started gobbling down his food with a plastic fork, then stopped, swallowed, and said, "Come on, eat. It's real good."

Laura Lee took a careful bite of the spicy crawfish in the rich reddish brown sauce. Then she made a face and spit the food back onto the plate. "Too hot!"

Caleb shook his head. "Well, at least eat the potato salad and the roll."

"You're gonna spoil that girl, babyin' her like that." Ryder, his wrinkled plaid shirt hanging outside his green work trousers, squatted next to the bench. "Eat that food and don't give me no back talk."

"It *is* too hot, Jack," Caleb intervened. "I can barely eat it myself. I wouldn't have bought it for her if I'd known how spicy it was."

Ryder scowled at his younger brother. "You shoulda got some American food like I did. These Cajuns are as bad as the Gooks over in Nam. They'll eat anything down here in these swamps." He took a big bite of his ham and cheese sandwich. Staring at Caleb's plate, he mumbled, "They probably got lizards and scorpions and such cooked up in that mess."

Caleb frowned. "Come on, Jack, give me a break, will you? I'm trying to enjoy my lunch. Besides, this stuff is really good." He motioned toward Laura's plate. "Why don't you try some? She ain't gonna eat it."

Laura held the plate out to her father.

"Get that stuff away from me, girl." He swallowed hard, took another big bite, and mumbled through a mouthful of meat and bread and cheese. "Did you see the money in that cash register when we paid? Musta been four or five hundred dollars in there."

Caleb peered over his shoulder at the cafe across the street. "Yeah, I saw it."

"They close at three," Ryder continued, glancing at the clock on the courthouse.

"Let's take it easy, Jack. Enjoy this nice warm weather a little bit. After we get settled in somewhere, I'd like to come back here on my motorbike and look the town over." Caleb glanced up at the October sunlight spinning like yellow smoke down through the live oaks. "Besides, we just got here. What's your hurry?"

"My hurry is we're running out of money."

An auburn-haired girl of about sixteen, wearing bell-bottomed jeans and a tie-dye shirt with a leather vest and matching headband, smiled at Caleb as she crossed the courthouse square. Holding his fork halfway to his mouth, Caleb smiled back, his eyes transfixed on the girl who was now glancing back at him over her shoulder.

The attraction was not lost on Ryder. "And you just git your mind off women, Romeo. They ain't good for nothin' but causin' trouble."

"Sure, Jack." Caleb kept his eyes on the girl as she crossed the street and disappeared into a clothing store.

"I mean it, Caleb." Ryder stepped in front of his brother. "We got to make some plans here. We got to git some money and git it real quick."

Laura had heard this kind of talk many times before and knew that it always led to the masks and the guns and the fast driving . . . and sometimes the noise and people getting hurt. She lost herself in her daydreams as she sat on the hard bench, eating her potato salad and roll and taking swallows of the sweet, fruity-tasting drink. The voices of her father and uncle droned on in the background, sometimes breaking through her reverie.

Laura Lee watched a group of people walking across the courthouse grounds toward the building's wide stone steps and towering white columns. Listening to the strange, musical language many of them spoke, she wished she knew what they were talking about and that she could speak as they did.

". . . only thirty minutes till they close for the day. We'll get all the money out of the till and be out of this place before they know what hit 'em."

A young blond woman in a long black skirt and white ruffled blouse pushed a baby carriage along the sidewalk. She stopped near Laura Lee, stooped over the carriage, adjusted the blanket, and returned the pacifier to the fretting child's mouth, all the while cooing words of love and comfort.

I wonder what kind of house they live in? Maybe it's big and white with a bedroom for the baby upstairs. I wish I could see all the little toys and teddy bears and things. I bet her husband wears a dress-up coat and a necktie when he goes to work like the people on television do. I wonder if she puts on a white apron in the kitchen when she fixes his breakfast?

". . . and then we'll park the truck on that side street. It's only half a block down."

"I'll be right back." Laura finished the last of her potato salad, slid off the bench, and walked over to a trash can next to the sidewalk.

Trotting happily down the sidewalk toward her, a black-and-gray terrier stopped and sniffed the air, then, its tail moving warily as though it was unsure of what kind of reception this small human would give it, took three cautious steps toward her.

"Hi, puppy. Want some roll?" Taking the roll off her plate, Laura dumped the plate into the can and squatted down, giving the dog a weak smile.

The little animal's tail fanned with doggish delight as it rushed forward and gulped down the remainder of the roll, then sat down as the girl scratched its ears.

"You're a nice little puppy." Laura Lee glanced warily over her shoulder at her father. "Don't you have a home? I wish I could take you home with me."

"Laura Lee Ryder!"

She flinched at the sound of her father's voice. The dog reared up when she quit petting it, placing its paws on her knees and whining for more.

"Leave that mangy mutt alone and git back over here!"

"Bye-bye, puppy." She gave the dog one last pet on its shaggy head and ran toward the two men who were still plotting and planning on the courthouse grounds, peaceful and pooled with shadow.

"Aw, quit your bellyaching, boy!" Ryder opened the door

of the pickup to let Laura out. "It's the best way to find out if all the customers are gone."

"She's just a little girl, Jack."

"She can do this much for her daddy," Ryder grunted, turning toward his daughter. "Can't you, baby?"

"Yes, sir."

Laura slid off the seat and onto the street. Walking to the corner, she turned and gave a backward glance, then continued on to the little cafe. When she opened the door a bell rang over her head, startling her.

"Don't be afraid, sweetie." A round-faced man in a big white apron sat at one of the tables covered with red-and-white-checked cloths. In front of him was a yellow legal pad and a stack of receipts. "It jis' let me know when a customer come in. Sometimes I'm back in de storeroom."

"Oh." Laura grinned. She liked the man immediately. His smile and the warm, friendly sound of his voice made her feel relaxed and safe.

"I'm afraid you too late for lunch." He glanced out the window. "You mama wid you?"

"No, sir. My daddy." She felt ashamed of herself, knowing that somehow she was part of a plan to do something wrong to this man. "I just wanted to use your bathroom."

"Sure t'ing." He pointed to a door leading to a dim hallway. "First door on de left."

"Thank you." She walked into the hallway, stopping in front of a door with a silhouette of a lady wearing a long, lacy dress and holding a parasol. Stepping inside, she breathed in the sharp smell of pine oil, then frowned at herself in the full-length mirror tacked on the wall. She pulled a paper towel out of its dispenser, wet it, and wiped her face clean. After brushing at her hair with her fingertips, she sighed deeply, flushed the toilet like she'd been told to do, and left.

"Come back when you got time to have lunch wid us, young lady," the smiling man said as she walked past him. "I'll give you a free bowl of ice cream for dessert."

Laura Lee felt a quick stab of guilt in her heart. Her cheeks flushed with the shame of what she was doing. Unable to hold the man's gaze, she put her head down and mumbled, "Thank you." As she pushed the cafe door open, the bell overhead jangled. This time its sound brought a welcomed sense of relief to be getting away from the place.

"Well," Ryder barked when she returned to the truck. "What'd you see?"

Laura Lee climbed up onto the seat and stared at the hamburger wrappers and crumpled paper cups on the truck's floorboard. "Just one man. He's sitting at a table with a bunch of papers."

"The fat one in the white apron?"

"Yes, sir."

Ryder stuck a blue steel .357 revolver inside his belt, buttoning his camouflage jacket over it. Then he shoved a roll of duct tape and a length of yellow nylon rope into one of the deep pockets of the jacket. "Come on, Caleb. This is gonna be like shootin' ducks in a barrel."

"No rifles?"

"No way, dummy!" Ryder growled. "This ain't no two-bit store way out in the middle of nowhere. There's people all over here, and maybe even a few cops."

"Why do you use that AK–47 so much, then?" Caleb asked with a guilty glance at his niece. "I mean like on that last job in Tennessee?"

"I had so many rounds fired at me from them 47s that it just feels good to get a few off at somebody else for a change." Ryder's laugh came out as a snort.

"That's not much of a reason, Jack."

Ryder's mouth became a thin line. "Only one I need, little brother. Anytime you don't like it, you're welcome to try to change the way I do things."

Caleb winced. "You think we need to wear this camo stuff?"

"Why not?" Ryder glanced nervously down the street. "It's

hunting season down here. We'll look like the local yokels coming right out of the woods."

"All right," Caleb agreed quickly. He slipped the .45 automatic under his belt at the small of his back. "Let's just get it over with."

Laura Lee watched them round the corner, hoping that the friendly man with the nice smile who had offered her ice cream wouldn't get hurt. Then she remembered something about angels from one of the Psalms that her grandmother used to read to her. Putting her hands together as she had seen other children do in Sunday school, she prayed: "Dear God, I ask you to take care of the smiling man in the cafe so he won't be hurt. And protect Uncle Caleb too." She took a deep breath, then finished. "And take care of Daddy."

Ten minutes went by, then she saw Caleb and her father walking briskly around the corner toward the truck. Her father carried the familiar brown paper bag in the crook of his arm, held firmly against his side like a halfback carrying a football on an off-tackle plunge.

"Git us outta here, boy." Ryder spat out the words as he slid into the passenger seat of the pickup. "Not too fast, now. I doubt anybody's going in that cafe with a Closed sign on the door, and I guarantee you he won't get loose from them knots I tied him up with."

"Daddy . . ." Laura Lee gazed ahead at the white frame houses with shade trees and gray-painted front porches as Caleb turned the truck onto a quiet back street.

"Yeah."

"The man didn't get . . . you know . . . hurt or anything." She stared at the floorboard. "Did he?"

"Nah." Ryder grinned at Caleb. "I chopped his feet off so he couldn't chase us. That's all."

Laura Lee turned wide, fearful eyes toward her father, her mouth open with unspoken words.

Ryder rubbed her head playfully. "Just kiddin', girl. Can't you take a little joke?"

"That's not much of a joke, Jack." Caleb braked at a Stop sign. "Which way now?"

"Straight ahead till you reach the bayou." He shook his head in disgust. "Turn right and then left on Highway 1 just past that old abandoned railroad bridge."

Laura Lee watched children walking, skipping, or riding bicycles along the streets and sidewalks on their way home from school. *Wish I could go to school. I wonder what they do there? Guess they read books, go to the cafeteria and eat lunch, and things like that. That little boy back home told me they get to go to the playground at recess.*

As they crossed the Highway 1 bridge, Laura Lee stood up on the seat and gazed down at the dark, placid surface of Evangeline Bayou. She saw a humpbacked, furry animal with tiny ears slip off the bank and swim toward the opposite shore. "Daddy, Daddy! Look over there! What is it?"

Ryder peered through the window. "Beats me. Looks like a big ol' rat, don't it?"

Caleb glanced at the bayou. "Nutria."

"What?"

"It's a nutria."

"How do you know what it is?" Ryder glanced back at the water-dark animal, leaving a soft, rippling V in its wake. "You ain't been in Louisiana no longer than I have."

"Read about 'em before we came down here. Bought a book about Louisiana in a rummage sale."

"Turn left here and follow right along the bayou." Ryder punched the button on the glove compartment and took out a crumpled road map. Squinting at it, he tapped it with the end of a thick forefinger. "This runs into Highway 77, and that'll take us to Interstate 10 at some place called Grosse Tete." He folded the map and stuffed it back into the glove compartment. "We'll find a place to spend the night after we put a little distance between us and that cafe back there in Evangeline."

Following the blacktop along the course of the bayou, the pickup passed fields of tall green sugarcane. Heavy trucks loaded with the purplish stalks roared past them on the way to the mills. Slowing down, Caleb took to the shoulder of the road to avoid a truck suddenly making a wide turn out of a field.

Laura Lee stared out the window at a gaunt-looking black man, gray haired and carrying a heavy walking stick that looked as though he had whittled it himself. He tipped his hat as they passed, then opened a mailbox and lifted out a thin stack of letters and a rolled-up magazine. Turning around, she watched him through the side window as he trudged down the long, dusty road toward a tin-roofed shack. *I bet his wife's cooking a big supper for him right now.* She watched smoke curling from a stovepipe sticking through the roof.

Laura Lee listened to the steady drone of the truck's engine, the whine of the tires on pavement as they crossed the Atchafalaya River Basin on the elevated portion of I–10. The world outside the truck's window looked like something out of a storybook. Bright moonlight glistened on the smooth surface of the lakes and bays, the willow islands and the cypress trees draped with long tendrils of Spanish moss silvering in the pale light. Oil rigs looked to her like spidery castles set down in the middle of this watery and mysterious landscape.

"Uncle Caleb . . ."

"What is it, sugar?"

"You think Daddy'll sleep for a long time?"

Caleb smiled at his niece. "Probably. He looked mighty tired when he went back to the camper."

She pointed toward the Basin they were traveling over. "It's pretty out there."

"It sure is," Caleb agreed, flexing his hands on the steering wheel. "I'm ready for a Coke and maybe a little snack. How about you?"

Laura nodded her head, a thin smile forming at the corners of her mouth.

"There's a little town just south of the interstate after we get across the Basin. It's called Breaux Bridge. I bet we can find a store there."

"It's not as big as the bridge we're on now, is it?"

Shaking his head, Caleb laughed. "No, baby. There's a little bridge over Bayou Teche. It used to be called La Pointe back in the 1700s because it's located at a bend in the bayou."

"How do you know things like that?"

"I like to read about the places where we are. Besides, there was a girl in my sophomore class from South Louisiana, and she told me a lot about this part of the country." Caleb shrugged the weariness out of his shoulders. "Nobody but the Acadian people lived around here for a long time. Back during the Civil War the Rebels burned the bridge so the Federals coming up the bayou couldn't get across to them."

Twenty minutes later Caleb pulled the truck into the shell parking lot of a rambling old clapboard building. A few curling slivers of yellow paint clung tenaciously to the weathered walls supporting a tin roof streaked with orange rust. The battered and fading sign above the front door proclaimed

R.D. Olinde, General Merchandise,

If We Ain't Got It—You Don't Need It.

"Looks like the place for us, don't it?" Caleb killed the engine and smiled at Laura Lee.

"Yep." She grinned back at him and slid across the seat, holding her arms out for him to help her down. She could do it herself, but it made her feel good to have her uncle lift her down out of the pickup's cab.

Holding tightly to Caleb's hand, Laura Lee entered the store. Four sixty-watt light bulbs hanging from the lofty ceiling by black cords filled the old building with a smoky light. It smelled of tobacco, cheese, plums, apples, coal oil, and the ineffable, inimitable fragrance of ancient wood.

To the left was a long counter with a large green cash register. In the glass cases beneath it and on the wall behind it, shelves held cigarettes, candy, packages of chewing gum, and a few toys and trinkets. A white plastic radio, perched on a rickety stool at the end of the counter, played John Denver's folksy hit "Take Me Home, Country Roads."

The tall shelves between the long aisles held canned goods, crackers, loaves of bread, as well as shoes and articles of clothing of every description and size. At the far end of the first aisle a porcelain and glass cooler gave off a blue-white fluorescent glow.

"What I can did for y'all?" A gaunt man with a gleaming bald pate fringed with white hair stepped out from behind a row of shelves. He looked like an old elf who had forgotten to put on his cap and pointy shoes. "Didn't mean to scare you, no."

Laura Lee motioned for Caleb to lean down, then whispered in his ear. "He talks funny."

"Shh . . . It's Cajun. Be polite, now." Turning back to the little man, Caleb said, "Yes, sir. We'd like to get a bite to eat."

"How 'bout some hoop cheese and salami?" Olinde offered, walking toward the back of the store. "Tastes mighty fine and sticks to yo' ribs too."

"I'll take your word for it. A pound of each, and we'll look around a little."

"He'p yo'self." He walked toward the back of the store with a spry step.

Laura Lee let her eyes wander to a shelf behind the cash register and found herself gazing at a Barbie doll with long blond hair who in turn seemed to be gazing back at her through the cellophane window of her box. She had once gotten one of the slim, elegant-looking little dolls for a birthday she could barely remember, but it had long since disappeared in the rolling bedlam of her travels.

Caleb placed two six-packs of Coke, a loaf of bread, a jar of mustard, and a pack of cinnamon rolls on the counter. "See anything else you want, runt?"

Laura shook her head.

Olinde dropped the sliced salami and cheese, wrapped in

brown butcher paper, on the counter. "Anyt'ing else I could get for y'all?"

"Guess that'll do it."

Olinde reached over and turned up the volume on the radio as the news reporter said, ". . . and got away with an un-determined amount of cash in the three P.M. robbery."

"We don't have many stickups around here, no," Olinde said as he began to ring up the groceries on his cash register.

The news reporter continued. "Evangeline Parish Sheriff Emile DeJean stated that no one was injured during the inci-dent. An eyewitness reported seeing two men wearing cam-ouflage clothing leave the cafe about the time the robbery oc-curred. . . ."

Laura Lee saw Caleb's eyes widen slightly, then his right hand lightly touched the handle of the pistol beneath his cam-ouflage jacket.

"Looks like we got 'dem robbers right here." Olinde grinned down at Laura. "I bet you really a midget dressed up like a little girl, ain't you?"

She glanced up at Caleb, then gave Olinde a shy smile.

". . . . The sheriff's office would release no further infor-mation on the suspects at this time."

"That'll be three eighty-five," Olinde said, placing the items in a brown paper bag. "Anyt'ing else?"

"Yeah," Caleb glanced down at Laura Lee. "Give us a half dozen Snickers and—" he thoughtfully rubbed his chin with his forefinger—"that Barbie doll up there."

3

CALEB AND BILLIE

Emile DeJean ran his hand through his curly black hair flecked with gray. Just under six feet, he had broad shoulders and a thick chest. One of his ancestors had sailed with the pirate Jean Lafitte, and Emile himself looked like a man who was never quite at home in a gray business suit or even in the twentieth century. "It's been two days now, Wilmer. You 'bout over the worst of it?" He sat behind his desk, cluttered with case files, scribbled notes, and correspondence, a white mug of steaming coffee in his hand.

"How you git over somet'ing like dat?" Wilmer Bourque, wearing a fresh white apron, his smile only a weak facsimile of the one that Laura Lee had seen in his cafe, fidgeted nervously in his chair next to the desk. "Dat man stuck his pistol right aginst my head and say he blow my brains all over de table if I give him any trouble. I was prayin' hard, me."

"Let's go over your statement again. I don't think you were talking too coherently the first time we took it." Dylan leaned against the sill of the window, sunlight streaming in behind him. He wore a long-sleeved navy shirt and khakis and held a legal pad and a yellow pencil.

"Co . . . what?"

"Coherent . . . clearly. You probably were still pretty upset about the robbery then."

"You right." Bourque nodded, his brow furrowed in concentration. "One was young, average height, five ten maybe, slim, sandy hair. He needed a haircut, but look like to me all de young men dese days need a haircut."

Dylan scratched on the pad, then smiled, noticing Bourque staring at his hair that hung over his ears and collar. "How old do you think?"

"Eighteen . . . twenty maybe. Dey wore dem masks and floppy hats, so I can't say for sure, but I don't t'ink he was no older den dat."

"And the other one?"

"Shorter, older, darker hair, t'irty maybe, kinda stocky." Bourque took a deep breath. "Mean eyes. He had real mean eyes, him."

Emile leaned back, the dry hinges of his swivel chair squeaking. "Anything else happen unusual?"

Bourque shook his head slowly. "Not dat I can t'ink of."

"Well, let us know if—"

"Wait a minute," Bourque broke in. "Dere was somet'ing kinda unusual, but . . ." He shook his head as though dismissing the thought. "Nah, forget it."

Twenty-five years in law enforcement before he had been elected sheriff the past year had taught Emile that sometimes square pegs did indeed fit into round holes. "Let's have it, Wilmer. Won't hurt to tell us about it."

"Well, about ten minutes before de robbery dis little girl come in to use de bat'room. I t'aught it was kinda funny she was all by herself."

"What'd she look like?"

Wilmer smiled, remembering how fragile looking and shy she had appeared. "Seven or eight years old, big blue eyes, and blond hair. Kinda skinny like she don't get nuttin' much to eat, her. Pretty little t'ing."

"Okay. Anything else?"

Bourque shook his head. "Looks like we gettin' bad as the

big city down here in Evangeline. Jes' last summer dat man wid de shotgun robbed my place."

Emile glanced at Dylan. "We were there, Wilmer. Remember, you had gone to the bank."

"T'ank the Lord for dat." Bourque expelled his breath as he rose from the chair. "But I ain't never gonna forget dat man lying dead on my floor."

Dylan saw again the black round holes of the shotgun's barrels, heard the thunder of the double barrel, saw the side of Emile's shirt erupting with red blossoms as he spun around in his chair, firing his snub-nosed .38 point-blank at the robber.

"I have some problems with that myself, Wilmer." Emile stood and shook hands with the little man. "Thanks for coming in. You've been a big help."

Wilmer nodded and, with a parting glance at Dylan's hair, waddled out of the office.

"What do you make of the little girl?" Dylan poured himself a cup of coffee from the pot on a table near the window, stirred in a spoonful of sugar, then took the chair that Bourque had been in.

"Probably nothing," Emile said with a shrug. He gazed at a cardinal perched in the crepe myrtle outside the window, its feathers glowing like embers in the morning sunlight. "That little girl doesn't belong to anybody from around here, though. That much I know for sure."

"Maybe just somebody passing through." Dylan sipped the rich, dark coffee.

"Could be. Lots of people traveling around these days." Emile's voice took on an edge of contempt. "Going to communes, 'turning on,' 'making love—not war,' and," he smiled ruefully and added, "trying to 'find themselves.' That's one I'll never understand."

"You sound like an old fogy to me."

Emile laughed. "Not quite, but I'm on my way. Right now I'm just a middle-aged fogy."

"Well, there's a good chance they're from out of state,"

Dylan suggested, "or at least not from *this* part of the state. What have we got?" He picked up Emile's pad and glanced at his notes. "Wilmer's descriptions . . . and maybe they've got a little girl traveling with them."

"Guess that's about it. Nobody we talked to saw them leaving, so we don't know how they're traveling."

After a quick rapping on the door, Elaine LeBeau, Emile's secretary, opened it and stuck her head in. "Got something you might be interested in."

"Well, let's have it."

Elaine had on her deputy's uniform complete with trousers and black boots. In her early thirties, she wore her deep red hair pulled back in a French braid. A scattering of freckles powdered her face. "Just came in on the wire from Morgan City." She handed Emile the sheet torn from the teletype.

Emile held the sheet at arm's length, squinted at it, then took a pair of black-rimmed reading glasses from his top desk drawer, put them on, and read the teletype. "Sounds like the same pair." He handed Dylan the sheet. "Camouflage clothing, but this time the short one used an assault rifle, probably an AK–47, instead of a pistol. No mention of a little girl with them, but it sure sounds like they're our boys."

"You really think they'd use a beat-up old pickup and camper to pull an armed robbery?" Dylan looked up from the teletype. "Maybe the witness made a mistake. He just saw two strangers in camouflage clothes, but he didn't see them leaving the lounge that was robbed . . . just saw them in the pickup."

"Could be. There's a lot of hunters from outside the parish down there this time of year." Emile loosened his tie. "They did their homework on this one, though."

"What do you mean?"

"The offshore workers spend a lot of money in lounges down there. They hit this one when the boys came off their seven days out on the rigs."

Dylan gazed down at the teletype. "It wouldn't take long

to find out the schedule. Anybody could apply for a job and get that kind of information."

"Or pretend they're looking for somebody on one of the rigs," Emile added.

"The witness didn't get the license number either." Dylan looked up at Emile. "All he noticed was that it had out-of-state plates . . . he thinks."

"At least we've got somewhere to start now."

Elaine picked up Dylan's tablet and the teletype he had placed on the desk. "I'll put these descriptions together with their M.O. and get it out to all units." Then she paused in the door and turned around. "Okay, boss?"

Emile glanced at Dylan, his face devoid of expression. "I think if something happened to me, she could run the whole show and nobody'd even know I was gone."

Grinning, Elaine said, "I'll take that as a yes," then turned and shut the door behind her.

———

The board-and-batten cabin stood on a narrow strip of land between the blacktop road and a bayou that bordered the trackless Atchafalaya Basin. A gallery running the length of the cabin faced the water and was connected to the dock by a single two-by-twelve. The dock in turn led back to a tin-roofed building that served as a garage and storage shed. A huge cypress tree rose from the grassy area between the shed and the cabin, providing a cooling shade during the blistering summer months. Red-eared bream and goggle eye fed beneath the graceful sweep of the willows that lined the banks.

"I almost wish we lived out here again, Susan." Emmaline DeJean, a short, vital woman in her late forties, stepped out onto the gallery and let her warm brown eyes wander across the bayou's surface, dark and glassy in the shade near the bank, wind-rippled and glittering farther out. Spanish moss, hanging in delicate tendrils from the cypress, lifted in the morning breeze.

"You can't have it back." Susan, wearing a white terry cloth bathrobe, followed her outside from the kitchen, a cup of steaming dark coffee in her hand.

"I said *almost*," Emmaline repeated, walking to the end of the gallery where an autumn-dry wisteria vine wound upward through a white trellis. Sitting down in a porch swing hanging by chains from the ceiling, she pushed off with her substantial legs and set it in motion. "Emile and I had our time out here when we were young like you and Dylan. I'm used to town life now. Never can tell when I'll have a Baskin Robbins attack. Besides, it's too far to the mall up in Baton Rouge."

Susan sat down carefully in a wooden rocker, one hand placed protectively over the mound of her stomach. "There was a time when I thought I could never live anywhere except New Orleans. But I wouldn't trade this little cabin for the finest house on St. Charles Avenue."

"From what Dylan says, you were raised in one of the finest homes on St. Charles Avenue."

"It's nice all right," Susan admitted, her gaze turning toward the past. "You can see Audubon Park . . . and I always loved the streetcars passing by, but it's nothing like this." She stared at the purple blossoms of the hyacinths along the water's edge, breathed in the cool morning air laced with the scent of wild flowers growing on the high ground just beyond the lattice, then watched a snowy egret lift off a piling that supported the dock and climb toward the tree line across the bayou. "No . . . nothing at all like this."

Emmaline brushed some crusty donut crumbs off her green-and-white-striped blouse. "If you like it so much out here, maybe we ought to just sell this place to you and Dylan."

Susan's serene expression changed to an excited glow at Emmaline's suggestion. "You really mean it?"

"We've been talking about it." Emmaline turned toward her own past. "Since we lost Robert over in Vietnam, Emile's kind of lost interest in the cabin. With Mary remarried now, we hardly ever see the grandkids, and Anne's never going to move back from New Orleans, so there's no one left to . . ." She paused, took a deep breath, then let the sentence remain unfinished.

"But it's been in Emile's family for such a long time."

"He thinks of Dylan as family," Emmaline said, then leaped quickly to another subject. "You and Dylan want to stay at our house in town till you have the baby?"

Susan noticed the concern on Emmaline's face. "No . . . no, I don't think so. Why?"

"Well, it's twenty minutes into Evangeline, and then a half hour to the hospital in Baton Rouge. You'd be closer, and then"—she smoothed an errant tendril of her short brown hair back into place behind her ear—"you just never know when a baby's going to decide it's time to see the world."

Susan smiled, grateful for the concern of a friend like Emmaline. "No, really, I'm fine. I've got the telephone, and then there's the two-way radio Emile lets us use so I can get in touch with Dylan anytime. You can do me one big favor, though."

"Sure."

"If things happen," Susan hesitated, "you know, real fast or something, be sure my parents get notified so they can be there when the baby's born."

"You don't see them much?"

"Only when I go down there."

"They still blaming Dylan for . . . for what happened to you up in Baton Rouge?"

Susan nodded and sipped her coffee.

"Well," Emmaline said flatly, "that's stupid!"

"They don't like my living out here either," Susan added. "They think it's not safe."

"Well, I guess they're probably right about that, anyway," Emmaline said, nodding her head.

"You really think so?"

"Certainly." She waved her hand in a sweeping arc. "Look at all these dangerous birds, ravenous rabbits, and ferocious fish. Yes, ma'am, you need to be down in New Orleans with those kindly ol' street thugs and dope dealers."

Susan laughed. "Maybe you ought to go down with me and explain it like that to them."

"Not me! I stay out of family problems." Emmaline sipped her coffee thoughtfully. "I can see why they might not have liked Dylan at first, though."

"Really?"

"Yep. When I first met him I didn't think he had a lick of sense."

"He probably didn't."

"Emile always liked him, though." Emmaline pushed off with her foot, setting the swing into motion. "Never would let me say a word against him."

"Even when his drinking got bad?"

"Especially then. He's always tried to see the good side of people." She sipped her coffee. "Unless they're the kind to hurt children. Then it's a different story."

"You mean like these robbers that bring that little girl along with them?"

"Dylan told you?"

Susan nodded. "They don't know it for sure, he said, but it looks like they use her sometimes to check out a place before they rob it."

"Wilmer told me she's a pretty little thing too. Poor and pitiful as a stray kitten, but pretty."

———————

Laura clung tightly to Caleb as they crossed the bridge over Evangeline Bayou into the town.

"You doin' all right back there, runt?"

She heard Caleb's voice whip past her in the wind. "Yes, sir. I'm doin' good."

"Just hang on and we'll be there in a minute."

Laura watched the late-breakfast crowd wearing business suits and carrying slim briefcases climb out of their cars and head toward the City Cafe before going to offices or the morning hearings at the courthouse. The earlier shift, traveling mostly in mud-splattered pickups, had worn work boots and jeans and carried their lunches in metal boxes or brown paper bags.

"Yeehaa!" Caleb shouted as they bounced over the tracks on Railroad Avenue. "Wasn't that fun?"

"Uh-huh," Laura muttered into the wind.

Turning left, they whizzed past the Five-and-Dime, a neighborhood grocery with fruit in wooden bins on the sidewalk, then slowed in front of a jewelry shop, its dark interior glowing with reflected light.

Laura Lee noticed the reason Caleb had slowed down. At the stop sign on the corner, a uniformed crossing guard with short iron gray hair pointed a warning finger at the young man on the motorbike.

"It'd be just my luck to get thrown in jail by an old woman," Caleb mumbled over the sound of the idling bike.

Laura watched the children, carrying books and brightly colored lunch boxes, walk and giggle and skip their way across the street. The girls wore neat dresses. Their faces glowed with health, and their hair shone shampoo-bright in the morning sunlight. *I wish I could go to school with them. I bet I could make good grades, and I'd sit up straight in my desk and pay attention to the teacher. I'd study real hard at home so I'd know the answers to all the teacher's questions.*

Caleb eased the bike through the intersection under the stern, watchful eye of the crossing guard. Then he drove carefully for several more blocks, parking on the courthouse square.

"Why did we come back here?" Laura scooted back on the bike's seat, sliding off onto the ground.

"I like this town. It's a pretty place to spend some time." He grinned at his niece. "Especially away from your daddy. He's getting too grumpy for me."

"Me too," Laura agreed quickly, then glanced around as though her father might be watching from behind one of the massive live oaks. She noticed that they had parked on the opposite side of the square from the cafe that Caleb and her father had taken the money from.

"You want some breakfast?"

Laura Lee nodded quickly.

Caleb reached into the back pocket of his Levi's and took out two flattened Snickers. Handing one to Laura Lee, he said, "Just pretend it's a big plate of ham and eggs."

"Okay." She pulled the wrapper open, folding it neatly back over the melted chocolate. Taking a bite, she chewed happily, content with her makeshift breakfast.

Caleb sat down on a stone bench beneath one of the live oaks and watched the activity around the courthouse square. Some people were on their way to work or to school or to shopping, and some were merely lounging around, the same as he and Laura.

"Is that your little girl?"

Turning around toward the voice behind him, Caleb suddenly stood up, staring at the same girl who had given him such a friendly smile his first day in Evangeline. She wore leather boots, freshly laundered bell-bottom jeans, and the same leather vest with matching headband. Her long auburn hair, parted in the middle, hung below her shoulders. "Uh . . . uh . . . no, she's not."

"Your wife, maybe. . . ?"

Laura Lee giggled, showing chocolate- and peanut-covered teeth.

The girl stepped around the bench, laid her books down, and knelt next to Laura Lee. "Well, you're not doing a very good job of taking care of her." She gave Caleb an admonishing glance. "A candy bar . . . for breakfast?"

"Well, uh . . . we've been on the road a lot lately, and, well, I guess our eating habits haven't been the best."

The girl brushed Laura Lee's tangled hair off her face with her fingertips, then turned back toward Caleb, an expression of longing mixed with envy on her beautiful face. "On the road a lot?" she repeated Caleb's words.

"Yeah, just traveling around, you know . . . seeing some of the country."

"Boy . . . I'd like to do that!"

"You would?" Caleb glanced around the square with its antebellum and Victorian architecture, pleasant and ordered and peaceful, the kind of town you might find featured on a calendar entitled "Gems of the Deep South." "Why would anybody want to leave a nice place like this?"

The girl looked at him with an expression of disbelief. "Boring! That's why. It's so *boring* here." She gave him a quick once-over with her eyes. "What's your name, anyway?"

"Caleb," he said, as though pleased he could remember it without giving it undue thought. "Caleb Ryder." He poked a hole in the air with his forefinger. "And this is my niece, Laura Lee. Her daddy's my brother."

"Hi. I'm Billie LeBlanc." She gave Laura Lee a pat on the head and sat down on the bench.

Caleb folded the wrapper back over his Snickers, tucked it in his back pocket, and sat down next to her. Then he leaned back and crossed his legs in an obvious attempt to act like an adult. "How come you're not in school?"

Billie turned and narrowed her eyes at him. "How come you're not?"

Caleb opened his mouth to speak, a half smile tugged at the corners of his mouth, and finally he merely shrugged. Then the two of them gazed into each other's eyes for five seconds before they both broke out into laughter.

"What's so funny?" Laura Lee, her mouth full of chocolate and peanuts, looked from one to the other.

"Nothing, baby." Billie grinned, taking her up onto her lap. "We're just laughing at nothing."

"You're really not in school?"

Billie kissed Laura Lee on her chocolaty cheek. "I really am, at least most of the time, except for first hour. It's gym class, and I get all mussed for the rest of the day if I dress out, so I just don't show up till second hour."

"Your folks don't mind?"

Billie shook her head. "They're so happy I go the rest of the day that they don't say anything about it." She glanced at Caleb's wrinkled shirt and Levi's with their slight crust of mud around the bottoms. "How about you? Your parents don't mind you running all over the country instead of going to school?"

"I already graduated."

"Yeah, I'll bet."

Caleb gave her a sheepish smile. "I really didn't graduate. But Mama and Daddy are both dead, so they don't say much about it one way or the other."

Billie hit him playfully on the shoulder. "That's a terrible thing to say." She seemed to fight the smile crinkling the corners of her hazel eyes. "It is kind of funny, though. Sometimes I wish my parents were more like that."

"What? Dead or quiet?"

She hit him again. "No, silly. I just wish they wouldn't try to run my life all the time."

"Sometimes I wish I had somebody to run my life. Half the time I don't have any idea what I'm doing."

"You wouldn't like it for long." Billie ran the tip of her forefinger across the back of Caleb's hand. "You know, you wouldn't look half bad if you were cleaned up a little. Couldn't you afford some new clothes?"

"Certainly. I got tons of money." Caleb shrugged. "I only dress like this 'cause I'm eccentric."

"I've got a great idea!"

"Oh yeah? I'm afraid to ask what it is."

"I'll buy you some."

"Some what?"

"Some new clothes, silly. Then you can take me up to Baton Rouge Saturday night to see Black Sabbath."

Caleb glanced down at his clothes, his voice laced with repressed anger. "There's nothing wrong with my clothes. Nothing a trip to the laundromat won't take care of." Looking back at Billie, the anger faded. "What's a Black Sabbath anyway?"

Billie was already making a habit of giving Caleb incredulous looks. "You never heard of Black Sabbath?"

"I told you, we've been on the road a lot."

"They're just the greatest heavy metal band in the whole world, that's all." Billie's voice held an edge of frustration. "They're going to be at Independence Hall up in Baton Rouge." She gave him two seconds to reply. "The tickets are only four dollars apiece."

"Oh."

"Well. . . ?"

"What is it with this *well*? Am I supposed to know what that means?"

"Do you want to take me?"

"Uh . . . yeah, sure. Why not?"

"Here's what we'll do, then." Billie took a lacy handkerchief from her pocket and began wiping the chocolate from Laura Lee's face and hands.

"She's getting candy on your shirt, Billie."

"Blouse, not shirt. And it's all right. I can always buy another blouse."

Laura lay her head on Billie's shoulder after the breakfast cleanup was finished. She already liked this young woman who had taken her onto her lap. Billie was clean and soft and smelled nice, and her hands were gentle. All these things made Laura think of her grandmother and the times she would take her onto her lap and rock her to sleep. She could barely remember those days. . . . They seemed like such a long, long time ago.

"Well, what do you think?" Billie stroked Laura Lee's hair as she continued laying out her plan for Caleb.

"I think we're gonna have a good time," Caleb said and grinned, "if your folks don't catch us."

4

SAINTS

Dylan strolled along the sidewalk toward Bayou Teche, coming to the old port where tradition held that Evangeline's boat docked beneath the ancient live oak that still bore her name. A bronze plaque in the little commemorative park told the story of Acadian exile and lost love:

Separated from Gabriel when the people of the village of Grand Pré, Acadia, were forced into exile by the British during the French and Indian Wars, Evangeline ended her long and perilous journey in St. Martinville. The Acadian lovers sought each other in vain and were reunited only when the aged Evangeline recognized Gabriel as a dying victim of the plague. To have all the years and all the miles apart end in such tragedy proved too much for her, and she succumbed to the shock of his death.

Sitting down on a wrought-iron bench in the little park, Dylan gazed at the old tree spreading its massive limbs out over the sluggish waters of Bayou Teche on one side and the new paved street on the other: the old and the new means of transportation in Cajun country. Above him, the afternoon sunlight shattered into a green-gold haze as it struck the leaves in the crown of the tree.

"How's your tennis game?"

Dylan turned toward the sound of a man's vaguely familiar voice, seeing him silhouetted in the dazzle of light behind him.

Then, looking downward, blinking into the glare, he recognized the scuffed combat boots. "Father Nick!"

"I'm glad to see you haven't forgotten me." The wiry little man in his black suit and clerical collar stepped out of the sunlight into the shaded brick walkway of the park.

Standing up quickly, Dylan shook the hand of his former teacher and tennis coach, clapping him roughly on the shoulder. "How could I forget you? I'd still be working on the New Orleans waterfront if I hadn't gotten that tennis scholarship."

Father Nick shook his head. "No. You'd have made it one way or the other, with or without me."

Seeing this thoughtful and steadfast man from out of his past, Dylan felt his youth rush back at him. The gray streaks in the priest's hair were new, but the same restless fire filled his eyes. "It's good to see you. I'd almost forgotten that my mother told me you'd been transferred to St. Martinville."

Smiling his inscrutable smile, Father Nick said, "Part of the aging process, I guess. The church is putting the decrepit old priest out to pasture."

"You'll never get old. You'll just die one day of too much concern for other people."

His laugh rang clear and clean as the autumn air. "Don't canonize me just yet, Dylan. I wouldn't be able to throw my occasional tantrums with the bishop if you dangle a Saint Nick medallion around my neck."

"I guess you could tuck it inside your shirt when you went to see him."

Father Nick chuckled, then sat down on the bench, crossing his legs, his scuffed boots giving him the appearance of a hobo who had stolen the clothes off a priest's back. His lean, dark face, light-dappled beneath the old oak, carried the detached and intense expression of one who has spent much time in solitude. "I've considered this on occasion, you know, during my thirty years as a priest."

"Considered what?" Dylan sat down beside his old friend, glad to be in his presence again.

"Sainthood. I'm reminded of Paul's letter to the church at Corinth, '. . . unto the church of God which is at Corinth, with all the *saints*.' That's what he called the believers, you see, *saints*. And he opens the book of Ephesians with '. . . to the saints which are at Ephesus . . .' and 'to all the saints in Christ Jesus which are at Philippi.' And on and on it goes."

Father Nick looked at Dylan as though expecting a comment, then shrugged. "You see, my old friend, at that time there were no mechanisms, no committee, no church body in existence to conduct the tedious and laborious investigation required to determine sainthood. That happened hundreds of years later." He gave Dylan another chance to speak, then said, "Yet Paul called *all* the church members saints. Didn't he?"

Nodding, Dylan noticed on closer inspection that the years seemed to have softened the light in Father Nick's wild, dark eyes. "I always pictured pious expressions and white robes and halos whenever I heard someone use the word *saint*."

"And so do most people, I suppose," Father Nick continued, "but the Greek and Hebrew terms translated *saint* in the Bible merely refer to someone set apart by God for His own."

A sense of peace seemed to fill the shady little park. Dylan felt it as strongly as he had in the presence of his grandfather, who had spent his life preaching the Gospel.

"And if we are to believe Jesus, the only way someone can become God's own is through His shed blood and resurrection. 'No man cometh unto the Father, but by me. . . . There is none other name under heaven given among men, whereby we must be saved.'" He turned toward Dylan. "That's what He said, isn't it?"

Dylan nodded his agreement, feeling somehow that the sound of his voice would disturb the something he felt in the air.

"It just seems logical to me, then, that every Christian is a saint in the eyes of God."

"But I thought you had to do miracles and go around praying all the time . . . things like that."

"Rules made by men, Dylan. Only God can make a saint, just as only God can make a Christian. No amount of work or prayer can save your soul. 'For by grace are ye saved through faith; and that not of yourselves; it is the gift of God: Not of works, lest any man should boast.' So you see salvation is not something you can earn; it's a gift you receive from God by faith in Jesus Christ."

Father Nick suddenly grew quiet, staring out at Bayou Teche's dark surface when a huge alligator gar broke the water near a clump of purple hyacinths, the scales of its great belly flashing a dull yellow as it rolled over and disappeared. The priest watched the ripples, still concentrating on his line of thought, then he continued. "Now, I'm not saying good works aren't part of the Christian life. James said 'that faith without works is dead,' and that our faith is shown by our works, but we don't do them in our own power. The Christian life is allowing Christ to do *His* works through our lives."

As Father Nick paused, Dylan said, "Whew! How did you learn so much scripture?"

"It's my business," he replied simply, then shook his head slowly back and forth. "Now look what I've done."

"What's that?"

"I've gone and preached you a sermon. That's what happens when the church assigns a man like me so many administrative duties it keeps him out of the pulpit."

"I probably needed a sermon anyway. It's been a while since I've heard one." Dylan glanced at Father Nick, thinking the priest might take the opportunity to chide him for not going to church.

But the priest jumped abruptly away from his scriptures. "Just look at you all dressed up in that uniform."

Dylan felt his face grow slightly warm. "I don't usually wear one, but I gave a safety talk at a school on my way over here, and the uniform seems to get the kids' attention."

"What brings you here anyway?"

"There's been a few armed robberies in towns near the

Basin. Looks like they're being done by the same people. Several of the sheriff's departments are working together—information sharing, that kind of thing."

"And what's going on in your life?"

Dylan felt the smile stretching his lips even before the thought formed itself into words. "Susan's going to have a baby."

Father Nick's dark face brightened considerably. "Hey, that's wonderful. Another little Dylan in the world. I'd better start praying right now."

Laughing, Dylan said, "Don't worry. I won't let him turn out like I did."

"You didn't turn out so bad," Father Nick said. "There were times back at Holy Name of Mary, though, when I had my doubts." He stood up, pressing his wild hair down with both hands. "Guess I'd better get moving."

Dylan stood up next to him. "I thought I'd buy you some lunch over at Thibodeaux's Cafe."

"I'd like that very much, but I have to be in a budget meeting at the church"—he glanced at his watch—"in five minutes. So good seeing you, Dylan. Let's get together another time and talk about the good ol' days down in Algiers."

"You've got a deal." Dylan shook his hand and watched the priest walk across the street toward a side door of St. Martin de Tours Church.

———

A white cloth and a plastic rose in a green vase decorated the table where Dylan sat in Thibodeaux's Cafe. Eating a bowl of seafood gumbo and freshly baked French bread, he gazed out the plate glass window at the sunlight gleaming on the church. He pictured Father Nick in some dim, musty office, nodding off to the sound of a soporific voice quoting figures from the parish budget. Then his mind turned back toward the years when this wild and gentle man had first come into his life.

Thud . . . thud . . . plonk. Thud . . . thud . . . plonk.

Helen St. John, her dark hair pulled back and tied behind with a blue ribbon, wore a blue print house dress and a white apron with tiny daisies on it. She stood at the back door of her white frame home in Algiers, directly across the river from New Orleans, gazing through the screen at the rear patio.

Palm fronds rattled in the breeze off the river. The scent of roses and gardenia moved in slow waves on the textured air, warmed by a blazing July sun. The sound had been steady for more than an hour: *Thud . . . thud . . . plonk.*

Helen watched Dylan, in his high-topped black Converse sneakers and cut-off jeans, hit a backhand against the stone wall of the patio, keeping his eyes fastened to the white ball as it bounced off the wall, hitting the uneven surface of the brick patio. As happened about half the time, the ball struck a crack between the bricks, bouncing at a crazy angle.

Moving his feet in short, quick steps, Dylan adjusted for the erratic bounce, changing to the forehand grip, his back-swing complete as he set up and stroked the ball. His eyes followed the flight of the ball as he bounced lightly on the balls of his feet, ready to play the next return.

Father Nick's scuffed combat boots looked out of place with his black suit and clerical collar. He stood five feet three and carried perhaps two teaspoons of fat on his 130-pound frame. His hair was wiry, black, and wild like his eyes. "The boy's got balance, good hand-eye coordination, and concentration. That's what most fourteen-year-olds don't have—concentration."

"After Noah was killed last year, Dylan found his old tennis racquet up in the attic and started playing with it almost every day." Helen gave Father Nick a sad smile. "I think it keeps something of his father alive for him."

"I tell you what I think, Mrs. St. John," Nick added, watching Dylan carefully. "I think I want your son to play on our school tennis team."

Helen gave him a thoughtful glance, then looked back at her son. "Dylan."

Dylan caught the ball in his left hand and turned toward the sound of his mother's voice. Sweat poured in rivulets down his face and arms and shoulders, soaking his thin white T-shirt. He squinted in the morning sunlight at the shadowy figures behind the screen.

"Father Nick's here to see you."

Nick watched Dylan walking toward them, dripping with sweat. "I think we'll have our visit outside if that's all right with you, Mrs. St. John."

"Surely." Helen beamed at her son. "He really likes you, Father. Whether you know it or not, you're sort of filling in for his daddy."

Nick nodded his head slowly, the light in his dark eyes as merry as an elf's as he pushed the screen door aside, walked across the porch and down to the patio. "You're gonna be another Tony Trabert the way you're hitting that ball."

Dylan combed his dark, wet hair back with the fingers of his left hand. "Yeah, I imagine ol' Tony lies awake at night worrying about me beating him at Wimbledon."

Nick laughed, his white teeth flashing in his dark face. "I don't know about Wimbledon, but there's a real good chance you could play on our school team."

Dylan shrugged and walked over to an ancient church pew made of heart pine, impervious to rot and insects. It sat on the bricks in the lacy shade of a crepe myrtle tree. He sat down, picked up a thick white towel, and mopped his face and arms.

Nick sat down on the other end of the bench. "I mean it, Dylan. You've got as much natural talent as I've ever seen."

Throwing the towel over his head, Dylan rubbed his hair briskly, then draped the towel across his knees. "I never had any lessons or anything."

"How did you learn the grips, then?"

Dylan glanced at Nick. "I just read about them in a library book. How could you tell I was making grip changes?"

"I played a little when I was in Jesuit High," Nick said, his face already glossed with perspiration, "and a little more when I went to Tulane."

"You played college tennis?"

Nick laughed, his elf eyes crinkling. "Nothing to write home about. Number six singles my junior and senior years. I had a 17–15 record as a senior." He took out a white handkerchief and wiped his face. "I'd just as soon not talk about my record as a junior."

"But college tennis . . . that's really something!"

Nick flinched at the sound of the screen door slamming. "Whew! I spent too much time in the Ninth Ward," he explained to Dylan. "That door sounded almost like a pistol shot."

Helen walked over to them carrying a metal Coca-Cola tray that held two glasses of iced tea. "I thought y'all might like something to cool you off."

"Thanks, Mama." Dylan took the tall glass, full of strong, dark tea and beaded with moisture, turned it up, and gulped half of it down. "Boy, that's just what I needed!"

After thanking Helen, Nick took a big swallow. "Just like my mama used to make."

"Well, I'll leave you menfolk to your visit." Helen fanned herself with the tray. "Too hot out here for me. I'm getting back to my window fan."

"You really think I can play on the school team?"

Nick held the cold glass against the side of his neck and smiled. "You could play number one singles for us this coming year if you'll let me help you with your game a little . . . and if you'll work hard. We'll have to spend a lot of time on the court. You need to practice your serve, forehand, backhand, volleys, then we'll play some practice matches."

"You got time for all that?"

"I'll make time," Nick said quickly. "We've got six or seven weeks until school starts. After that I'll only have a couple of hours on Saturday mornings, and one or two days we can hit an hour or so right after school lets out."

Dylan's eyes grew bright with excitement. "You really think I'm good enough?"

"I didn't say that."

Dylan's face took on an expression of bewilderment mixed with disappointment. He stared down at his black tennis shoes, soaked with sweat.

"What I said," Nick went on, "was that you have as much talent as anybody I've ever seen." He took a long swallow of tea, then set the glass on the brick patio next to the bench. "Tenacity is the next most important part . . . and the rarest. Then you've got to be able to put it all together under the pressure of match play."

"Then maybe I won't make it."

"That's a possibility," Nick said flatly. "But it's something we can find out together."

Dylan lifted his eyes toward Nick. His face had brightened instantly. "That's good enough for me."

———————

" '. . . kneeling beside him, kissed his dying lips, and laid his head on her bosom. . . .' " As he spoke the words, Dylan watched a full-grown bobcat, its sharp ears etched in the sunlight, step into the deep shade of the forest on the other side of the bayou and vanish like tawny smoke.

Susan, wearing a light cotton sweater over her orchid-colored maternity dress, sat next to her husband in a folding aluminum chair webbed with nylon. "That's so sad," she said in a hushed tone. "I'm not sure I want to even guess the poet."

"The title will do, then."

"Does it get better?"

In answer to his wife's question, Dylan continued the poem. " 'All was ended now—' "

"It doesn't, does it?"

" '. . . the hope, and the fear, and the sorrow.' "

"You know I don't like poems with unhappy endings. I don't want to play."

Dylan merely grinned at her. " 'All the aching of heart, the restless, unsatisfied longing—' "

"Wordsworth!" Susan cut him off.

"You *always* guess Wordsworth."

"I do not!"

"Who is it, then?"

"Yeats."

"That's the second one you always guess."

"It is not! I told you I don't want to play." Susan placed her hands on the swell of her stomach and looked away. "It's too sad . . . and I'm old and fat and ugly."

"Don't talk like that, sweetheart; you're not old." Dylan shielded himself with his arms as he spoke.

After a one-second pause, Susan turned in the chair as quickly as her condition allowed and began pummeling him with her small fists. "You think you're so funny . . . don't you?"

"Longfellow." Dylan flinched as one of Susan's flailing fists slipped through his guard, catching him a glancing blow on the cheek. "Longfellow!" he almost shouted.

Susan stopped, slightly breathless. "What are you babbling about now?"

Carefully, Dylan lowered his guard. "The lines are from Longfellow."

"I should have known."

"Known what?"

"It's *Evangeline*, right?"

"Yes . . . it is, but why should you have known?"

"You went to St. Martinville today." Susan settled herself back in her chair, smoothing her dress. "Evangeline and Gabriel; Evangeline Oak on Bayou Teche; the statue on the church grounds. You came home, looked up the poem, and memorized a few lines." She gave Dylan a knowing smile. "Then you come out here and act like it's something you just pulled out of the air."

"Curses, foiled again."

" 'What a tangled web we weave' "—Susan wove an imaginary web in the air before her, then raised one eyebrow toward her husband—" 'when first we practice to deceive.' "

"What can I say?" Dylan bowed his head in mock regret. "You caught me in the act. I did wrong, and I omit it."

"You what?"

"I omit it."

"You mean you *ad*mit it?"

"Is *that* the word?" Dylan shook his head sadly. "No wonder I've had so much trouble all these years. I've been *o*mitting all my wrongs when I should have been *ad*mitting them." He looked at Susan, nodding sagely. "This could be a whole new life for me."

"You're insane."

"And you're absolutely beautiful!"

Her husband's abrupt change of direction caught Susan off guard. "How can you say that? I'm a mess and you know it. Just look at me."

"Who's kidding whom now?" Dylan took Susan's face in his hands, kissing her tenderly on both cheeks, then her lips. "You've got that . . . that glow about you. Maybe all pregnant women have it and I just never noticed it before." He gazed directly into her clear green eyes. "Absolutely beautiful."

Quick, bright tears formed in Susan's eyes. She brushed them away, then leaned forward, placed her lips on Dylan's, and gave him a lingering kiss.

"Whew!" Dylan huffed as she pulled back. "That's some kiss, little mother." He took a deep breath. "You'll never guess who I saw today."

"The sheriff of St. Martin Parish."

"Come on. You already knew that. I saw Father Nick."

"No kidding. How's he doing?"

"Never changes," Dylan said, smiling at the memory of his old friend. "He just looks a little older, that's all. Hasn't put on a pound, though."

"He's in St. Martinville permanently now?"

"Yep. I think he really likes it too. His mother's side of the family are all Cajuns, and St. Martin de Tours is the mother church of the Acadian people."

"I knew that."

Dylan grinned at his wife's impertinent expression, then continued. "So he ought to feel right at home over there." He rubbed his chin thoughtfully. "I'd like to get together with him once or twice a month for lunch . . . maybe just a cup of coffee."

"I think you should too."

Layers of clouds, their edges painted shades of peach and lavender by the vanished sun, floated beyond the tree line across the bayou.

"He preached me a sermon while we were sitting in that little park down by the bayou today."

"Maybe he thought you needed one."

"You're probably right." Dylan stared at the changing colors of the sky. "I'm sure glad I met him. I might be at the bottom of the river today just like . . ."

Susan knew her husband's thoughts. "I think you should call Father Nick tomorrow and set up a time for y'all to get together. He and Emile . . . the two of them might just straighten you out."

Dylan laughed and leaned back in his chair. "It was a great October, wasn't it? Warm and dry. I have an idea we'll pay for it this winter, though."

"Who cares? We'll just stay inside our little cabin and drink hot chocolate and listen to old music." Susan reached over and took her husband's hand. "What happened at your meeting today in St. Martinville?"

"Half a dozen sheriffs' offices sent people there. Everybody seems to think these latest robberies are being pulled by the same two thugs."

"How are y'all going to find them?"

"The plan is to scour the whole perimeter of the Basin to

try to find an out-of-state camper with the two men and the little girl. It'll turn up sooner or later."

"I think it's a shame the way they bring that little girl around with them when they rob people."

Dylan closed his eyes, breathing deeply. "It could make for some real problems when we catch up to them. I just hope we can take them when she's not around."

"Surely a father wouldn't put his little girl in danger by having a shootout with her right in the middle of it."

Dylan let Susan's statement pass, folding his hands on his stomach, feeling relaxed after the long day. Then he opened his eyes and watched the last of the light fading over the Basin.

"You ready for supper?"

"I guess so."

Susan stood up, gazing down at her husband who had closed his eyes again. "Well, are you going to get up?"

"Nope. Feels too good here."

"We're having crawfish bisque with pecan pie for dessert."

Dylan stood up and put an arm around his wife as they walked together across the dock toward their cabin. On the other side of the bayou, an owl glided above the darkened forest, beginning the hunt, its passing as silent as the floating clouds.

5

BLACK SABBATH

"You expect me to ride on this . . . this reject from a junk-
yard?" Billie wore her usual bell-bottom denims and leather
accessories as she stood with hands on hips glaring at Caleb's
motorcycle.

"What's wrong with it? I washed the mud off the fenders."
Caleb had bought a brown leather jacket to wear with his Levi's
because it matched Billie's vest.

"Well," Billie tossed her head, her long hair billowing
around her face, "I'm certainly not going anywhere on *this*
thing!" She whirled around, facing the courthouse, its white
columns glimmering in the last rays of the daylight.

"Guess I had you figured all wrong." Caleb threw a leg over
his bike and sat down.

Billie whirled again. "And just what do you mean by that,
you grubby hillbilly?"

Caleb remained calm in the teeth of Billie's verbal attack.
"I thought you were hip . . . that's all. You know, like the girls
in *Easy Rider*."

"I am!" Billie insisted. "I'm as hip as anybody *you've* ever
known!"

"I *thought* you were." Caleb shook a cigarette from a pack
of Marlboros and stuck it in the corner of his mouth. "But
you're not. You're square."

Billie, finding herself speechless in the face of the supreme insult, felt hot tears welling up in her eyes. "I'm . . . I'm not," she wailed. "There's nothing wrong with wanting to look nice . . . to keep my hair from getting all mussed up."

Caleb gave her his tomcat-with-a-cornered-mouse grin. "I think it would look just gorgeous blowing in the wind. I can see it now." He made a movie director's screen with his hands. "You sittin' on the back of the bike, hair streaming out behind like a comet, and us riding free and easy down the highway."

Billie smoothed her hair down with both hands. "You don't think I should wear a scarf?"

"What? And hide all that beautiful long hair? Not on your life, babe."

"Well, all right. I guess it wouldn't hurt to try it just this one time." Billie fitted her purse strap snugly over her shoulder, hitched her leg over the backseat, and climbed on behind Caleb, locking her arms around his waist.

"What time you gotta be home?"

Billie shrugged. "My dad says midnight, but I haven't been in that early on Saturday night since I was fourteen. Let's just see what happens."

"Now you're talking." Caleb flipped up the kickstand, revved the engine to life, and roared off around the courthouse square, heading north out of town. Crossing Evangeline Bayou next to the old, rusting iron railroad bridge, he traveled along Highway 1, paralleling the west bank of the Mississippi.

Soon they were in the midst of the clattering, clanking frenzy of Cinclare Plantation's grinding season. Tall tractors towed rubber-tired buggies piled high with sugarcane from the nearby fields. Flatbed trucks roared past them on the highway, hauling the harvest from outlying areas to the sugar mill. Stalks of crushed cane littered the blacktop and the dirt side roads.

Caleb pulled over to the side of the highway, parking next to a coulee lined with reeds and cattails. He stared at the huge bulk of the sugar mill, rising out of the dark surrounding cane fields. Clouds of smoke rose into the night air from the mill, lighted for round-the-clock operation. "Don't they ever knock off work?"

Still seated on the back with one foot on the ground for balance, Billie said, "Nope. Twenty-four hours a day, seven days a week till they get the harvest in. They've got to beat the first freeze."

"That's some job they've got!" Caleb stared again at the mill, the play of light and shadow on its towering metal walls and the sharp angles and turns of its roof, smoke rising into the night, backlighted and billowing in the wind. It looked like a medieval scene somehow come back to life in the twentieth century: serfs and peasants in their gasoline-powered oxcarts, all serving the lord of the corrugated metal castle.

"I thought we were going to a concert."

"Oh yeah . . . sure." Caleb revved the bike's engine, waited for an opening in the heavy traffic of sugarcane trucks and weekend fishermen, hauling bateaus and bass rigs behind their pickups, then shot forward, leaving a shower of white shells behind him.

Caleb took Billie's arm as they left Independence Hall, which was located between Capitol Lake and the Mississippi River and next door to the Lakeshore Hotel. The exiting crowd wore mostly bell-bottoms and tie-dyes, sandals and leather boots, while others wore an assortment of ethnic and folksy fashions including the American and Eastern Indian peasant look with feathers, fringes, and beads. The pungent smell of marijuana drifted on the chill night air.

"How'd you like it?" Billie's face was bathed in a Black Sabbath afterglow.

"If that music had been any louder, they'd have been getting complaint calls from Ohio."

"You didn't like it?"

Caleb picked an open spot between the traffic winding

along North Third Street and pulled Billie across with him. "I couldn't understand a word."

"That's not important."

Stopping on the other side of the street, Caleb asked, "What *is* important, then?"

"You've got to *feel* the music." Billie placed her left palm flat on her chest.

Caleb led the way toward the lower parking lot of the Lady of the Lake Hospital where he had left his motorbike. "My eardrums must know what's important, then," he muttered. " 'Cause they're still *feeling* the music."

"You just don't understand their music or the heavy metal message they're trying to get across," Billie insisted. " 'Iron Man' is a great song."

"If you say so."

"I don't even know why I came to the concert with you. I thought you were the one who's supposed to be hip."

"Hip's got nothing to do with music."

"What does it have to do with, then?"

"A person's lifestyle. Not being tied to a nine-to-five job, then coming home to a nagging wife and screaming kids." Caleb found himself rattling away, words spilling out that sounded strange in his own ears; words that he knew deep inside were as foreign to what he truly believed as the music of Black Sabbath. He would have given anything to trade places with Billie, to live in a real home in a town like Evangeline. "The way you handle yourself."

"You don't sound too convincing to me."

Caleb glanced back at the jumble of cars and vans trying to get out of the parking lot at the same time. "Let's wait till this traffic clears out a little before we head home."

"Sure."

Taking Caleb's hand, Billie walked with him across the parking lot to the shoreline. In front of them, the lighted 450-foot limestone tower of the state Capitol lay its reflection down across the smooth, dark surface of the lake.

"That's some building!" Caleb stared at the Capitol, rising against the night sky.

"Tallest capitol in the country," Billie said proudly. "Earl Long built it when he was governor."

"Nice weather down here too." Caleb put his arm around Billie's waist. "Warm in the daytime; cools down just right at night. Just perfect."

"It'll change."

"You mean it actually gets cold down here in alligator and cottonmouth country?"

"You'll see." Billie watched the traffic creeping along on the west side of the lake, then she stepped away from Caleb and gazed into his eyes.

"Something wrong?"

"Just what are you doing down here anyway?"

"What do you mean?"

"Don't answer a question with a question."

Caleb picked a white shell up from the edge of the parking lot, then threw it out into the lake. "I already told you. Just traveling around. Seeing some of the country."

"Where'd you come from?"

"Tennessee."

"How do you live?" Billie's voice took on an edge. "I mean, I never hear you talk about work or anything like that. Where does your money come from?"

"Well, I didn't want to tell you this," Caleb mumbled, his head down, "but if you insist."

"I insist."

"I'm really with the FBI doing undercover work."

Billie whirled around and started walking briskly across the parking lot toward the street.

Catching up to her, Caleb took her by the arm. "Come on. I was just teasing."

Folding her arms across her chest, Billie glared at him once, then gazed out at the traffic.

"All right. All right!" Caleb began leading her gently back

toward the lake. "You see," he began, not truly knowing where to begin. "We've had some pretty rough times in our family. Daddy got killed at the lumber mill while Jack was over in Vietnam." He glanced at Billie, wondering if she believed that he was in fact telling the truth this time.

"You're through with all this joking around about everything this time . . . right?"

Caleb nodded and continued, not thinking ahead, just letting his words roll out. "And then after Jack came home, his wife, Wanda, she finally just up and took off."

"She left her baby?" Billie's eyes grew wide at the thought of a mother actually abandoning her own child. "Laura Lee's her little girl, isn't she?"

Caleb looked at the shock in Billie's eyes, envying her world that was apparently without the heartaches that were so much a part of his. "Yeah, Wanda's her mama. But don't be too hard on her. Jack ain't the easiest person in the world to live with . . . since he got back from Nam, anyway."

"Poor little thing."

"That ain't all," Caleb said, determined to finish his discourse one way or the other. "About two years after Wanda left, Mama died, and that 'bout did it for our family."

"What do you mean?"

"I mean she was the only thing left in our family. . . ." Caleb stopped, shaking his head slowly back and forth. "I guess I don't know what I mean."

"Go on," Billie said softly, slipping her hand inside his. They had reached the shore. A breeze from the river swept across the lake, causing the lights of the Capitol and the hotel to shimmer on its dark surface. "You can tell me."

"Well," Caleb began again, "Mama always looked out for Laura Lee . . . Jack and me, too, I guess. But it was more than that, more than just taking care of all of us." He took a deep breath, letting it out slowly. "She just had this way of making you feel, I don't know . . . good about yourself, I guess." He glanced at Billie. "You know, like you were special."

Staring at Caleb's sad, vulnerable face, Billie suddenly thought of an old movie she had seen starring Steve McQueen. "Did you ever see the movie *Baby, the Rain Must Fall*?"

Caleb shook his head. "Why?"

"Oh, no reason really. It was about a country boy trying to make it big in the music business. Just wondering if you'd seen it." Billie smiled, seeing in her mind's eye Caleb in the part McQueen had played. Laura Lee even looked like the little girl who had played his daughter, and even though she was Caleb's niece, the characters in the movie had already become to Billie almost interchangeable with Caleb and Laura Lee.

"Well, that's my story."

"What kind of work did you say you do?"

"Huh?" Caleb felt a sudden hot flush of shame rising in his chest. "Oh . . . just odd jobs—you know, this and that—anything to put some bread on the table. We, uh . . . got this job out on the rigs we go to sometimes."

"And you're all three living in that little camper on the back of your brother's pickup?"

"Yep."

"Isn't it awfully . . . crowded and, well, you can't have any privacy or anything."

For the first time Caleb felt embarrassed at the deplorable circumstances of his life. Until he had met Billie, life on the road had seemed one adventure after the other. Now he saw himself as a hobo, a bum, someone with no future and nothing to offer anyone, especially someone like Billie. "Aw, this is just temporary. We're gonna get us a real place to live as soon as we get some money saved up."

"Where?"

Caleb let his imagination take over. "Oh, I don't know for sure now. Maybe a houseboat out in the Atchafalaya Basin. They say it's real pretty out there."

"Gee, that'd be such fun! Living in a houseboat." Billie's face lighted with excitement. "Almost like . . . Robin Hood." She grinned at Caleb. "The Basin would be our—I mean your

74

hideaway instead of Sherwood Forest."

Caleb felt a tingling of anxiety at how close Billie had come to the real thing. "Yeah, except we don't rob the rich and give to the poor like he did."

"Oh, I know that, silly!" She gazed at the amber and gold lights in the lake, then up toward the heavens. "What I wouldn't give to live that way . . . even if it was just for a little while. Just to get away from everything that's so . . . so conventional." She glanced at Caleb. "So . . . predictable."

"I know just what you mean," Caleb mumbled, envying Billie's safe, secure, predictable life.

———————

"Why not, Jack?" Caleb sat in the shade of a willow at the bottom of the levee on the western edge of the Atchafalaya Basin. "I'm tired of living in this cramped little camper." He grinned at Laura Lee. "Wouldn't you like to have a real house to live in for a change, runt?"

Chewing on a bite of a McDonald's cheeseburger, she mumbled, "Uh-huh."

Jack sat in the cab of the truck, door open, his legs hanging off the edge of the seat. He took a bite of a Big Mac and washed it down with swallows of Dixie Beer from a can, spilling some on his already food-stained Dickie's work shirt. "You might have come up with a good idea for a change, boy."

"No kidding?" Caleb seemed surprised that his older brother actually agreed with something he said.

"Not because this ain't good enough for us, though"—he jerked his thumb at the camper—"but because the law's bound to find us if we keep using this truck. It's a dead giveaway with the camper and Tennessee license plates."

"And it's not gonna outrun a police car if they get after us," Caleb added.

"They could near 'bout catch us on foot." Ryder chuckled in a rare show of good humor. Then his brow furrowed in concentration as he continued. "This place down here ain't like the mountains with hundreds of little back roads where no-body hardly ever goes. All them hills and hollers was just per-fect for hidin' from the law." He turned up the Dixie can, fin-ishing it in two gulps. "I 'spect that's why the moonshiners used to give them federal boys such fits."

"We got a lot better place to hide down here than the mountains, Jack."

"Yeah. Where's that?" Ryder grabbed a "church key" from the dashboard and popped two holes in another can of beer. Foam dripped down the sides onto his hand.

Caleb pointed eastward, sweeping his hand around toward the south. "Out in the Basin."

"That's not funny," Ryder said, taking a swallow from his can. "This is serious business here."

"I *am* serious."

"What do you think we are . . . tadpoles?" Ryder's good humor was vanishing as rapidly as his second beer. "There ain't nothing but bayous and lakes and backwaters out there."

"That's why it's perfect."

Ryder glared at his younger brother. "I've had about enough of this, Caleb!"

"A houseboat."

The expression in Ryder's eyes changed from incipient anger to bewilderment to sudden interest. "A houseboat . . ." He drained the can, tossing it on the ground next to the first. "You jist might be on to something there, little brother."

"It's perfect." Caleb's voice rang with the excitement he always felt at the prospect of a new experience. "There's thousands and thousands of acres out there in the Atchafalaya Basin for us to hide in. And the pipeline canals are everywhere . . . just as good as the roads back in the Tennessee mountains. They'll take us anywhere we want to go."

"Kinda hard to drive down a pipeline canal, ain't it?" Ryder gave his brother a half grin. "Looks to me like the en-gine would keep flooding out on you."

"You got no imagination, Jack." Caleb stood up, his actions

becoming more animated. "First we sell the camper, rent a houseboat, then we buy a bateau—"

"Hold it," Ryder interrupted. "Jist hold on. What in the world's a *bat toe*?"

"Bateau, b-a-t-e-a-u. It's French for boat. Down here they're flat-bottomed fishing boats . . . usually made out of aluminum."

"Oh."

"We'll get one with a pretty good-sized motor, tow it behind the houseboat till we find a good place to tie up . . . you know, real secluded and all the way back in the swamps. Then we just use the bateau like it was a car to get us back and forth."

"Sounds good except for one little thing."

"Yeah, what's that?"

"What happens when we get back to dry land in this *bat toe*?" Ryder sneered. "We just drive it out on the blacktop and head on down the road or what?"

Caleb glanced at Laura Lee, noticing again the bruise above her left eye that he had first seen on her the morning after his date with Billie. "Why don't you go inside the camper and play with your doll for a little while, sweetheart?"

"Okay." Clutching her cheeseburger in one hand, she climbed up the fold-down steps into the camper.

"What was that all about?"

"I . . . I just didn't want her to hear any more," Caleb said sheepishly.

"You got some strange ways, boy." Ryder punched two holes in the top of another beer and took a long pull on the can. "It's the way we make our living. How you gonna keep her from finding out what's going on?"

"She don't have to hear me say what I'm gonna do," Caleb said defensively, "and she's never actually gone inside with us when we pulled a job either."

Ryder glanced toward the camper, then gave his brother a sardonic smile. "She's gonna have to grow up someday; find out this is a mean ol' world. The sooner the better, I say."

"Anyway," Caleb hurried on, trying to ignore his brother's comment. "I'll steal us a car, and we'll rent a shed to keep it in somewhere on the edge of the Basin. Somewhere we can dock the boat when we come in to . . . to pull our jobs."

"Sounds like you figured it out pretty good, little brother." Ryder took a pack of Camels from his shirt pocket, shook one out, and stuck it in the corner of his mouth. "Now, here's how we'll work it. You drive this rig to New Orleans and sell it. There's car lots down there that'll buy it no questions asked."

"Why New Orleans? Other than it being a good place to sell the truck easy?"

Ryder flicked a kitchen match with his thumbnail, let the sulfide flash into smoke and flame, then lit his cigarette. " 'Cause there's so much crime there, one more car theft ain't gonna make no difference to the local cops. Not like it would here in these little towns around the Basin."

"What's the difference?"

"Steal one here and it's likely to belong to some cop's brother or cousin or at least somebody they know, then they put a lot of time in trying to find it." He took a hard pull on his cigarette, letting the smoke curl through his nostrils. "Steal one in New Orleans and the boys in blue ain't gonna bother looking for it too hard. 'Bout the only way we'll get caught is if we do something stupid like gettin' a traffic ticket. Then they'll run the license number and find out the car's stolen."

"When you wanna do it?"

"Right now." Ryder got out of the truck, took the remainder of his six-pack, and sat down under the willow, leaning back against the trunk. "You take the girl with you, sell the truck, and by then it'll be dark and you can get us a car."

"Why do I have to take her?"

Ryder took a swallow of beer, closed his eyes, and smiled. "You come up with a good idea . . . then you ask a stupid question like that." He shook his head slowly from side to side. "Because you ain't gonna look very suspicious to the cops if you got a kid tagging along with you. That's why."

"I'd rather go by myself."

Ryder opened his eyes. Anger sparked in their depths, anger that could quickly flare into rage. "You do exactly what I tell you, boy. And do it now!"

———————

"That man gave us a lot of money, huh, Uncle Caleb?" Laura, shivering slightly in the chill that came with sunset, walked out of the used-car lot next to her uncle. She held tightly to his hand, glancing at the passersby, many of them seedy-looking men with stubbly beards and mismatched clothes.

"Yep. Fifteen hundred dollars," he said and grinned broadly. "The man said he already knew somebody who was looking for a truck and camper, so he could sell it first thing in the morning. They like to make deals like that."

As they walked along the street, Laura gazed at the old stucco or wood frame houses with concrete porches painted gray, and tiny, cluttered yards crowded with loud children and barking dogs. Most of the streetlights were out, and some of the automobiles had been stripped of tires and anything else of value and sat rusting into the gutters. She clutched tighter to Caleb's hand. "How are we gonna get back to Daddy?"

Caleb had rehearsed his story on the drive to New Orleans. "Easy. I'm looking for a car that belongs to a friend of mine. He said it's around here somewhere."

"I didn't know you had a friend here."

"I got lots of friends, Laura Lee."

As they walked along the sidewalk, Laura saw that the blocks ahead grew brighter. Soon the amber glow of street-lights made her feel warm and secure. Houses were much larger now, painted in pastel colors with wide, wooden porches holding rocking chairs and gliders and swings suspended on chains from the tall ceilings. Huge shade trees stood above manicured lawns with flower beds and trimmed hedges.

"It's pretty here," Laura said in a hushed voice, as though

speaking in church. "Do you think we could live in a house like this one day, Uncle Caleb?"

"Maybe. Would you like that?"

"Yes, sir. I sure would."

Caleb patted her on the head. "Well, I guess I'll just have to get to work and buy us one, then."

Laura followed him along a side street, dark with shadows. Windows glowed with the blue-white light of television sets. Through a window she saw a family of five seated at a table having supper. One of the children, a girl about her age, giggled at something her father leaned over and said to her.

"There's his car." Caleb pointed to a dark green Ford sedan parked on the street next to a tall hedge, shielding it from the owner's house. He glanced up and down the street, then walked the short distance to the end of the block and looked both ways. "Yep, this is the one, all right."

"It's pretty. Why is he giving it to you?"

"He's just letting me borrow it, sweetheart." Caleb slipped a long, thin screwdriver from out of the inside pocket of his leather jacket and walked around to the driver's side of the Ford. Inserting the screwdriver into the small space between the frame and the glass of the vent window, he pried the locking lever forward, then pushed the glass inward.

"Don't you have a key?"

Caleb squeezed his arm though the vent, his fingers barely reaching the lock button. "He lost it, but he said it would be all right if I took it like this." Straining to hold the lock between the tips of his fingers, he pulled the button upward, unlocking the door. "Now, that wasn't so bad."

Laura sat down on the curb, watching her uncle open the door, pull a penlight from his pocket, and stretch out on the car's floorboard. Pulling her yellow sweater across her thin chest as the dampness sent a chill through her, she heard the squeak of a screen door opening on the other side of the tall hedge. "Uncle Caleb, I think somebody—"

"Don't bother me now, Laura Lee. I'll be finished with this

in a minute." Caleb pulled several rubber-sheathed wires from beneath the dashboard near the steering column, sorted through them, selected the ones he was looking for, and touched their exposed ends together.

Laura stood up as the Ford's starter began to grind with a whining noise. She saw Caleb holding the wires and depressing the car's accelerator with his free hand.

"Hey, you! What's going on out here?"

Laura jerked her head toward the sound of the man's voice as he stepped around the corner of the hedge. Wearing a white undershirt, gray trousers, and black house slippers, he had a round belly, a head of thick white hair, and gripped the handle of a heavy shovel with stubby hands.

Suddenly the engine caught, sputtered once, and roared to life as Caleb revved it up with his hand on the accelerator.

"You stealin' my car, you dirty, sneakin' thief!"

"Uncle Caleb!" Laura started for the car, took two steps and tripped, falling on the rough concrete of the gutter.

Caleb slid quickly out of the car, grabbed Laura Lee beneath the arms, and tossed her bodily over to the passenger's side of the front seat. Then he whirled around just in time to confront his attacker.

"I'll bust yo' head, you rotten . . ." The man aimed the shovel at Caleb's face in a wild roundhouse swing, using all the force of his arms and short, heavy body.

Caleb ducked beneath the shovel as it banged off the top edge of the open car door. As the man's momentum carried him around, Caleb, uncoiling his legs and turning his shoulders into the blow, hit the man a staggering right to the jaw. His knees buckled and hit the pavement, the shovel clanging down on the curb. He managed to get to his knees, but Caleb crouched down and landed another right squarely on his chin. The man's eyes glazed over, he clawed at something in the air that only he could see, and toppled over on his back.

Bending over the man, Caleb saw his chest rising and falling. Relief flooded through him that the man was still alive. As he stood up he saw that lights were coming on in several houses nearby. He jumped behind the wheel, slammed the door, and jerked the transmission down into drive. Reaching the corner, he turned down another side street and disappeared into the night.

PART TWO

———

Safe Thus Far

6

THE OLD WAYS

"Billie's run away before. I know that better than anyone."
Judge LeBlanc, tugging at his cherry red tie every few mo-
ments, paced back and forth in Emile's office. "But this time
it's different." His close-cropped gray hair, jutting chin, and
dark, glinting eyes gave the impression of a Marine colonel
leading the charge onto a South Pacific beachhead.

"What's different about this time, Judge?" Emile sat on the
edge of his desk, idly tapping the eraser of his pencil on the
back of his hand.

LeBlanc stopped, a look of defeat crawling steadily across
his chiseled features. "This time she took a lot of clothes and
other things with her. The other two times she just took off in
the middle of pitching a fit."

"You think she means to stay gone this time?" Dylan wore
a khaki shirt with two button-flap pockets, Levi's, and brown
leather boots. He poured coffee into a thick white mug and
handed it to LeBlanc.

"Thanks." LeBlanc sipped the coffee, his eyes staring over
the cup's rim at the traffic passing on the street outside the window. "I'm afraid she does."

"Have you or your wife had any disagreements with your
daughter lately?" Dylan studied the expression on the judge's
face—a mixture of grief, fear, and anger.

LeBlanc's bitter laugh turned into a snort. "Not more than fifteen or twenty times a day."

"More severe than usual?"

"No . . . not at all." He took a deep breath, letting it out slowly. "In fact, things seemed to be going a little smoother for the last day or two."

"Did she take her makeup?"

LeBlanc looked puzzled. "Why . . . why, I believe she did. Is that important?"

"It means you're probably right. I expect she means to stay gone for a while this time." Dylan had learned from past experience working with runaways that it was best to be upfront with the parents rather than trying to sugarcoat the facts so that they would go down easier.

LeBlanc's face seemed to sag as though his aging process had suddenly accelerated. "But how can you know for sure? How can you be certain that—"

"Dylan spent some time working in Juvenile Services with the State, Judge," Emile interrupted, counting on his years of friendship with LeBlanc to give him confidence in Dylan also. "He's seen a lot of these kinds of cases."

"You can never be certain what's going on in the minds of kids this age," Dylan continued, hoping to come up with any piece of information they could use to find the judge's daughter. "She may be back home already, but there are certain signs you can look for."

"Like taking makeup along?"

"Yes, sir. Girls almost always put that near the top of their list." The grief in LeBlanc's eyes caused Dylan to turn away. He gazed out the window at the familiar cardinal perched on the slick tan limb of a crepe myrtle. Its crimson feathers seemed on the verge of bursting into flame in the morning sunlight. "For boys the priority seems to be taking something along for self-defense. Pistols are usually the weapon of choice."

LeBlanc shook his head quickly as though trying to clear it of thoughts that had become intolerable. "We've got to find her! Are you going to notify other law enforcement agencies so they can be on the lookout?"

"Elaine's putting the information on the teletype right now," Emile explained.

"What else can we do?"

"Why don't you have a seat, Judge." Dylan motioned toward a chair next to Emile's desk.

"Might as well, I guess," LeBlanc admitted reluctantly. "This pacing isn't doing me any good."

"We'll need you to make a list of your daughter's close friends." Dylan handed him a legal pad and a pencil. "Especially any new boyfriends you might know of."

"You might want to write down her hangouts, too, Judge," Emile added. "Somebody at one of them might give us a line on what's happening with her." He motioned for Dylan to follow him outside. "We'll leave you alone till you're finished. You'll probably think better without us distracting you."

The judge mumbled something under his breath as he wrote on the pad in his small, neat script.

"I knew that girl was going to take off sooner or later," Elaine said as soon as Dylan had closed the door behind him. "Anybody could see it coming."

Emile walked over to the coffee service next to the wall and poured a third of a cup. "Maybe you could fill us in on some of the details, Elaine. I think we're going to need all the help we can get on this one."

"No discipline." Elaine finished writing a note on a slip of paper and speared it on the slim spike of her message holder. "Billie got everything she wanted all her life. . . ." She folded her hands on her desk. "Except her mama and daddy."

"The judge is in there right now"—Emile nodded toward his office door—"going through the torments of hell because this girl's missing, Elaine."

"I didn't say they don't love her." Elaine's face saddened as she spoke. "Maybe women notice things like this more than men. But when you see a sixteen-year-old girl out on the streets as much as that one, something's wrong."

"Her daddy took the Corvette away from her after that last time she left."

Elaine shrugged. "You know as well as I do, Emile," she continued in a soft voice, "that when the judge isn't on the bench he's out at his hunting camp in the Basin, or playing bourée with the boys, or saltwater fishing down at Grand Isle."

Emile glanced at his office and nodded.

"And his wife's so busy out trying to save the world with her charities and benefits that she can't see she's losing her own daughter."

Sipping his coffee, Emile sat down in a wooden chair next to Elaine's desk. "Well, all of that may be true, Elaine, but it isn't helping us find Billie."

"That's why I started in on all of this, I guess," Elaine said, shaking her head slowly. "Got so carried away with the sound of my own voice, I almost forgot what I really wanted to tell you."

"Well, let's have it."

"A week ago, maybe longer," Elaine began, "one morning when I was running a little late, I saw Billie talking to some boy out on the square. He was sitting on a bench on the opposite side of the square from Paw Paw's Cafe."

Emile placed his coffee cup on the desk, leaning forward, his expression grown attentive. He refrained from asking Elaine questions, knowing that he could depend on her to give him all the helpful information she could remember.

"He was about six feet tall, slim, sandy hair . . . maybe eighteen or nineteen, a little older than Billie, anyway." She rubbed her chin with the tip of her forefinger. "He was a nice-looking kid but kind of . . . I don't know, rough looking, I guess you'd say. His clothes were wrinkled and a little dirty, like maybe he didn't have a mother looking out for him."

Emile glanced over at Dylan, who nodded at him. "Could you tell if he was in a car or truck, any indication of how he was traveling?"

Elaine shook her head slowly, then stopped. "Wait a minute! There was a motorbike parked on the curb pretty close to where they were."

"Anybody else with him?"

"Yeah, there was." Elaine nodded. "I remember thinking it was kind of strange at the time. A little girl who should have been in school at the time."

"About seven, blond hair, blue eyes, kind of dirty—pretty little girl but skinny?"

The expression on Elaine's face answered Emile's question.

"You're going to have to update that teletype on Billie LeBlanc already, Elaine," Emile said.

"Jim Bowie and Jean Lafitte. That's some team, isn't it?" Emile loosened his blue-and-gray-striped necktie, savored the rich, spicy smell, then added Tabasco to his large-sized bowl of gumbo.

"Were they really involved in the slave trade together down here?" Dylan asked, brushing flaky crumbs of French bread off the tan shirt of his deputy's uniform.

"That was just one of their more profitable enterprises. Lafitte sailed his ships up Bayou Lafourche and traded anything that would put a dollar in his pocket."

"Thibodaux's *still* a pretty interesting place." Dylan gazed out the restaurant's plate glass window next to their table at the endless field of sugarcane tilting in the November wind. "Where else could you find a restaurant all by itself out in the middle of a cane field?" He grinned at Emile. "Sometimes I think it's time to get out of Louisiana, then something like this comes along and I decide maybe I'll stick it out a little longer."

"Yep," Emile agreed, "it's the restaurants in the cane fields that make life worth living." He glanced at a huge John Deere cane harvester lumbering toward them down the shell road. "Better enjoy the view of the cane field while you can. It won't be there much longer."

Dylan took a bite of his oyster po'boy, crispy and chewy at the same time, the briny, tangy taste of the sea blending perfectly with the fresh tomatoes, lettuce, and shallots from the rich Louisiana farmlands. As he gazed at the harvester turning into the green cane fields, his thoughts returned to the reason for their trip down to Thibodaux. "You think anything was accomplished at the meeting this morning?"

"Maybe." Emile shrugged. "My experience with meetings is, about all that's accomplished is deciding when to have the next meeting." He turned toward Dylan. "That's if it happens to be real productive."

"Sounds like my years in state government."

"Sounds like any bureaucracy." Emile placed his spoon down on the heavy white plate his bowl rested on. "But I think we all agreed on one thing this morning, and it couldn't have happened if all the sheriff and police departments in the Basin hadn't been involved in this investigation."

"The bad guys aren't staying anywhere on the Basin's rim, or somebody would have found them by now."

"Exactly. They've either moved somewhere deep inside the Basin, or they've left this part of the state."

"Well, we'll know one way or the other pretty soon," Dylan said, watching the harvester plow its cumbersome way through the cane field.

"Right. Three or four days is the longest they've gone without committing a robbery."

Dylan nodded, his mind turning toward the possibility of danger for the child who had been traveling with the two robbers, and now perhaps the judge's daughter, when they confronted them. "You think we ought to tell the judge there's a chance Billie might be with the men we're looking for?"

"I don't know." Emile stared thoughtfully out the window, his dark eyes a mirror of concern. "I'd rather be more certain she's with them before we say anything."

Dylan glanced at a nearby couple. The man in his mid-twenties, wearing a lime green polyester leisure suit, seemed enthralled over his date's mood ring. "I don't think there's much doubt about it, Emile."

"Why's that? She could be anyplace."

Shaking his head, Dylan explained, "She's only been gone overnight before. With girls like Billie, it's usually just a matter of time until they find the right boy to hook up with."

"The right boy?"

"Yeah. Most girls seem to feel they need somebody to look out for them before they hit the road. And in Billie's case, it's not likely to be somebody from Evangeline."

"You think maybe the boys from Evangeline don't measure up to her standards?"

"That's got nothing to do with it," Dylan answered. "But who's going to take a chance on getting caught with the judge's daughter? What kind of treatment do you think they'd get when they went before him in court?"

"Yeah, I see what you mean." Emile rubbed his chin reflectively. "Funny, I didn't even think of that. Must be getting old on the job."

"Besides, in a small town like Evangeline, the boys are all old hat for Billie. She'd be looking for somebody different, exciting, not her usual high school friends."

"You're probably right," Emile agreed reluctantly. "The night marshall's seeing this guy drop her off early last Sunday morning on his motorbike pretty well cinches it. I guess we'd better let the judge in on this when we get back."

"I wish we'd come up with some kind of plan this morning where all the deputies and police officers in the Basin could work together on catching these guys."

"Everybody's pretty territorial around here," Emile offered by way of explanation. "We can all agree that boiled crawfish are necessary for the survival of the Cajun culture, and that fishing and hunting and beer drinking are our God-given heritage." He watched the young couple get up and head for the door. She wore Earth shoes and a long black trench coat.

"Probably on their way to one of those Transcendental Meditation centers."

"You're starting to sound like an old fogy again."

"I told you, not for another decade or so," Emile shot back. "Since I don't meet the age requirement, I'm merely old-fashioned." Shaking his head, he turned back toward Dylan. "Anyway, getting a dozen or so Cajun police and sheriff's departments to agree on a single course of action is about like asking the KKK and the Black Panthers to get together and come up with a solution to the country's racial problems."

"Come on. I thought y'all stuck together."

"We do. But in this line of work every town has its own way of doing things. Cajuns are an independent bunch. Had to be to survive when the British kicked us out of Nova Scotia." Emile glanced out the window as an empty cane buggy bounced along the rutted road behind a tractor. "One sheriff usually passes his mantle of power down to somebody he's groomed for the job while he was still in office—his chief deputy, the chief of the detective division, or maybe even his own son."

"So the old traditional way of doing things gets handed down from one generation to the next."

"That's about it. We're making a few inroads into modern methods," he admitted, "but like everything else down here, the old ways die hard."

Dylan thought of the sleepy little river town of Evangeline—the friendly people, dependable, hardworking, and hard playing; and the traditions, the way of life they had held fast for 250 years. "That's it."

"That's what?"

"That's why Susan loves Evangeline so much. You just said it. 'The old ways die hard.' " Dylan thought of a line from one of his favorite poems, a poem he had first heard in a driving rainstorm on an old abandoned wharf across the Mississippi River from New Orleans: . . . *I strove to love you in the old high way of love.* . . .

"So even if we are a bunch of hicks and hayseeds," Emile said with a smile, "bumbling around trying to solve crimes like the Keystone Cops, you'll put up with us anyway?"

"I think I just might."

Emile fished a ten-dollar bill out of his wallet and dropped it on the table. Scraping his chair back on the floor, he stood up and said, "Well, let's go, my good man. The horse and buggy awaits."

———

"What're you stoppin' here for?" Ryder, the pockets of his green fatigue jacket holding the ninety-two dollars he had taken at gunpoint from a bar owner in Grosse Tete twenty minutes earlier, scowled at his brother. "We're already taking the long way back to the houseboat."

Caleb pulled into the parking lot in front of an old clapboard building with a faded sign that read R.D. Olinde, General Merchandise. He killed the engine and zipped his leather jacket. "It's starting to turn cold, Jack. I want to buy Laura Lee a coat."

"In a grocery store?"

"This fella's got everything you can think of in his store." Caleb took the .45 automatic from his belt and shoved it under the seat. "You can wait here if you want to. I won't be long."

"Nah. I might as well git me a six-pack as long as we're stoppin'."

Caleb glanced at the handle of the .357 Magnum protruding from his brother's belt. "You don't want anybody seeing that thing, Jack. Why don't you leave it in the car?"

Ryder buttoned his jacket over the pistol. "I feel like I'm half naked without it."

As Caleb crunched across the white shells behind his brother, a slight shiver rippled through his body. *It's not that cold*, he thought, glancing upward. Only a few hours ago at the houseboat, he had seen a pale, thin sliver of moon hanging among the stars. Now dark clouds, rolling in from the northwest, covered the vast dome of the sky. He heard the chill wind moaning in the lofty eves of the ramshackle old building and the first heavy drops of rain pinging against its tin roof.

Stepping inside, Caleb squinted into the smoky light that filled the old building and smelled the same unmistakable fragrance he had smelled here before.

"I'm gonna get the beer," Jack said, heading toward the far end of the first aisle where a porcelain and glass cooler gave off a blue-white fluorescent glow.

"Okay."

"Can I help y'all wid somet'ing?" The gaunt man with a bald head fringed with white hair and gleaming dully in the weak light stood behind a long counter to the left.

"No, thanks." Caleb grinned as he turned away, thinking that Olinde still looked like an old elf without his cap and pointy shoes. Walking across the heart-pine planking of the floor, worn smooth over the years by countless customers, he glanced at the tall shelves separating the long aisles. They held canned goods, crackers, loaves of bread, cans of shoe polish, and a varied assortment of kitchen and bathroom items.

Olinde returned to his work of stacking packs of Juicy Fruit chewing gum in the glass case beneath the counter. He hummed along with the Beatles' latest hit, "The Long and Winding Road," playing on a white plastic radio perched on a rickety stool at the end of the counter.

Caleb continued on to the far wall of the store and began sorting through a stack of clothes in the children's section. He selected a bright red wool coat with a fur collar. Inspecting the quilted lining, he said out loud, "This ought to keep her warm this winter."

"Pretty too."

Caleb hadn't seen the man in the murky light and shadows of the old store. Short and slim with wild, dark hair flecked with gray, he wore a tan topcoat. His eyes gleamed with a kind of wildness, too, but one that had been tempered and tamed by . . . by what Caleb could not have said, although he sensed

94

no threat from this stranger with the open, honest smile. "I think she'll like it."

"For your daughter?"

"Niece."

The man held up a dark green work coat, made of a heavy canvas-like material, durable and inexpensive. "What do you think about this one?"

"Not very stylish," Caleb said candidly. "But it looks like it'd be hard to wear out. Warm too."

"It's perfect, then."

"For you?"

"No," the man said, nodding as though he could see the intended owner of the coat already wearing it. "It's for one of our parishioners. He spent all his money on his wife and kids after he lost his job, and now that he's back at work he's got nothing to keep himself warm this winter."

"Nice of you to help him out."

"Just part of the job." The man glanced at his watch. "Well, it's getting late, and since you approve of my selection, I think I'll go and pay for it."

Caleb liked this man instinctively and thought of asking what kind of job he had that brought him out so late at night to buy a coat in a country store, then he remembered what he and his brother had done in the barroom at Grosse Tete only a few minutes before. He decided to keep his own counsel, picturing the look on Laura Lee's face when he handed her the new coat as he followed the man back toward the front of the store.

"Put that thing away!"

The voice of the man with the wild, dark hair had taken on a ring of authority as Caleb looked up from admiring Laura's new coat. For the first few seconds his mind refused to accept the signals his eyes were sending it. His brother was swinging the barrel of his pistol around toward the coat buyer, who stopped on the other side of the counter from Olinde.

Then Ryder took two quick steps backward so he could keep both men in his sights.

"Forty-tree years I been runnin' dis store and I ain't never been robbed." Glaring at Ryder, Olinde slammed the drawer of the heavy green cash register shut with a clanging sound. "You ain't gonna be de first, no."

Ryder pointed his revolver at Olinde's frail chest. "Open that drawer and give me all the cash or I'll—"

"Jack, don't do this!" Caleb heard the sound of his own voice as though someone else were speaking the words.

"Shut up!" Ryder flicked the gun barrel toward Caleb. "Whose side are you on, anyway?"

"Listen, if you're down on your luck, we can help you." The slim man placed his coat on the counter with a slow, deliberate action. His voice had grown calm, taking on a soothing quality. "I've got a few dollars you can have."

"Let's have it, then."

The man took his wallet carefully out of his back pocket and placed it on the counter next to the coat. "It's yours. I'd appreciate it if you took the money out and left the wallet, though."

Ryder glanced at Caleb. "Git that wallet!"

Accustomed to taking his brother's orders instantly, Caleb picked up the wallet, took a twenty and three ones out, and placed it back on the counter.

"Twenty-three dollars? That's all you got?"

"That's it. I'd give you more if I had it."

"All right, old man," Ryder growled, pointing the pistol at the little man's head, his finger tightening on the trigger. "Open that cash drawer or I'm gonna open up yore skull."

Olinde stood his ground, his bony chin jutting toward Ryder like the blade of a plow. "I ain't scared of you, no. You t'ink robbin' people make you a big man, you. You ain't nuttin' but a scared little boy hidin' behind dat gun!"

Color rose in Ryder's face. His eyes bulged. Bellowing with rage, he rushed Olinde, swinging the pistol in a sweeping backhand motion. The revolver's barrel caught the little man on his right temple, splitting the skin. His faded eyes glazed over as he crumpled to the floor.

Caleb saw the next events only as a blur of motion. The slim man with the wild hair seemed to suddenly appear on the other side of the counter next to his brother, his left hand fastening around Ryder's wrist in a viselike grip, pushing it downward and away from him. Ryder grunted with effort trying to free his gun hand, then, with a bellow of pain, he dropped the pistol. A fraction of a second later the pistol bounced on the wooden floor, the man's right fist slammed against Ryder's jaw, sending him reeling backward into a counter. He lay on his back among a jumble of toys and trinkets he had jarred loose from the shelves.

Transfixed by the sudden violence, Caleb saw the man disappear behind the counter as he crouched down where Olinde had fallen.

"Mr. Olinde, are you all right?"

Caleb watched his brother struggle to a sitting position, crawl quickly forward, and snatch the pistol from the floor. Shaking his head quickly to clear it, he stood up. Then, clutching the pistol with both hands and extending his arms, he pointed it downward toward the floor behind the counter.

"Jack, don't!" As though in a soundless dream, Caleb watched the pistol leap four times in his brother's hand, fire spurting from the dark, round hole in the barrel. Then the noise of the exploding shells and the sharp smell of cordite seemed to hit him all at once. He felt completely numb, unable to move. His chest constricted as though a giant hand had gripped him, squeezing the air from his lungs.

A memory flashed at the back of Caleb's mind like an old black-and-white movie, flickering and indistinct . . . their last robbery in the mountains. The terrified face of the storekeeper after he had fired his old single-barrel shotgun, staring at the AK–47 in Jack's hands. Jack had loosed a quick burst above the man's head to keep him down until they had made their getaway. But this . . . this was something different . . . this was . . .

Caleb saw his brother leap behind the cash register; heard the loud ching as the No Sale sign popped up in the glass window; saw him snatching bills from the cash drawer, stuffing them into his pocket, then run around the counter.

"What are you lookin' at?" Ryder grabbed Caleb by the arm. "We gotta get out of here."

Caleb heard a low moaning sound from behind the counter, then the sound of someone moving on the floor, attempting to rise, then collapsing. Taking two careful steps, he stopped and gazed down at a pair of scuffed combat boots, splayed outward, as motionless as if they had been on the feet of a department store mannequin. One painful step more and he saw blossoms of a startling crimson color forming on the tan raincoat of the wild-haired man and on the white apron of R.D. Olinde.

"I said come on!"

"We—we've got to do something!" Caleb felt his brother pulling him toward the door.

"We gotta *leave*. Now!"

Then they were outside the enfolding warmth of the old store and into the cold, windswept November rain. Caleb plodded across the wet shells of the parking lot gleaming in the weak amber light from the store. He didn't feel the heavy drops pounding him, plastering his hair to his skull, turning his clothes sodden and cold and heavy against his body.

"Hurry up, boy!"

Caleb stared at his brother yelling at him from behind the steering wheel of the car, its door open, engine running, and headlights cutting twin glaring swaths through the darkness, gleaming on the silvery, angling rain. He felt as though nothing around him held any true substance or form; that he had been suddenly swept away into a world of ghosts and wraiths and nightmares that had no end.

"If you don't get in this car, I'll put a bullet in you!"

Coming back to the world of night and blowing rain, Caleb gazed into his brother's bottomless, strange eyes and knew with absolute certainty that he meant every word.

7

THANKSGIVING

Dylan pulled off the blacktop into the tin-roofed shed next to the bayou. Turning off the engine of the blue Volkswagen, he sat in the gloom and breathed in the dampness and the musty smell of the building, listening to the rain drumming on the tin roof. He thought fondly of the indolent October days, dry and warm and filled with a golden light. Now the first of the winter storms had begun in this late November twilight.

Through the doorway that opened toward the water, Dylan watched the rain beating on the weathered boards of the dock and dancing on the bayou's surface. Beyond, on the opposite bank, the tops of the trees swayed in the wind.

Getting out of the car, Dylan walked beneath an aluminum bateau hanging from the ceiling joists and past a ten-horse Mercury outboard screwed tightly to a two-by-four nailed to the wall. Hunting and fishing gear, most of it belonging to Emile, cluttered the shelves and hung from sixteen-penny nails driven into the walls. Slipping through the side door, he ran along the shell path that led past the dock to the gallery of the cabin.

"Goodness, you're soaked!" Susan wore a blue maternity dress and a pale yellow sweater as she stepped onto the gallery and handed Dylan a towel.

"Thanks." Dylan rubbed his dark hair briskly, wiped his

face and neck, and cleaned his boots on the doormat. "Looks like we're in for a long, wet winter."

"Fine with me as long as it doesn't get below freezing more than two or three times. Come on in and let's get you out of those wet clothes." Susan took the towel, kissed him on the lips, and stepped back into the kitchen.

In the kitchen, with its Formica dinette and yellow-and-white-checked curtains, Dylan sat down and took his boots off, then his uniform. He slipped into thick cotton socks, gray sweat pants, and a long-sleeved white pullover with *LSU Tennis* in purple letters on the front. Susan walked over from the stove and placed a mug of steaming hot chocolate in front of him.

"You read my mind."

Susan sipped from her cup of milk-whitened hot tea. "Nothing like it to warm you up when the first real cold front comes through."

"You're not having any?"

"I . . . I just don't feel like something quite that heavy. Tea's more to my liking tonight." She brushed his damp hair back with her fingers. "My mother called this morning."

"Yeah," Dylan muttered into his mug. "What's happening on the New Orleans social scene?"

Ignoring the question, Susan said, "She and Daddy are going"—she glanced at the clock on the wall behind Dylan—"well . . . they've already left now for Bermuda."

Dylan thought how his mother would hardly leave the house and take a chance of missing the phone call now that Susan was this far along in her pregnancy, but he decided to let it remain merely a thought. "Business trip?"

"It's all right, Dylan," Susan said, reading her husband's mind, "the doctor said I'm not due for another week. They'll be home in plenty of time."

Dylan, deciding to steer the conversation away from Susan's mother, leaned over and kissed his wife on the forehead. "How're you feeling?"

"Like your maiden aunt," Susan frowned, "when you kiss me like that."

Smiling, Dylan placed his fingertips along the smooth curve of her chin and kissed her warmly and lingeringly on the mouth. "Is that better?"

"Much," Susan sighed, "and to answer your question, I'm feeling just like Humpty Dumpty did before he fell off the wall."

Dylan laughed, then sipped his chocolate. "Humpty broke," he said, placing his cup on the table. "You're just going to have a baby . . . and then get your schoolgirl figure back again."

"Let's hope it doesn't take all the king's horses and men to get me together again."

"I think a doctor and a couple of nurses can probably handle the job for you."

"Seafood gumbo in one hour," Susan said, standing up and turning toward the counter. "Why don't you turn the television on. *The World of Charlie Company* is on channel 9 tonight."

Dylan watched his wife as she lifted the lid on the gumbo pot, stirred it with a wooden spoon, then began dicing pecans on the cutting board. "That's about a reporter who follows a rifle company around in the boonies for a month or two, isn't it?"

"I think so."

"Might be worth watching." Sipping his chocolate, Dylan took pleasure in seeing Susan make the preparations for sweet potato casserole, cornbread dressing, and the other Thanksgiving Day treats. Taking a last swallow, he stepped behind Susan, pushed her soft, dark hair aside with the backs of his fingers, and nuzzled her on the slope of her neck.

"Hmmm . . . that's nice." Then she turned and shooed him out of her kitchen. "You go and watch your program now and let me get this cooking done. Emmaline and Emile are expecting us at twelve sharp tomorrow."

Walking into the living room, Dylan turned on the television and sprawled on the sofa. The images on the screen began to clear, coming into focus as the picture brightened. He stretched his body out full length on the couch, feeling a great weariness settle over him.

The red sun settled like a huge, flaming wafer beyond the wide, flat expanse of rice paddies and earthen dikes. Dylan stood at the edge of a triple-canopied forest, gazing upward at the medevac circling down, down, downward through the lavender twilight. The heavy throp . . . throp . . . thropping of its rotors always proved a comforting sound to him and the other Marines in his company. It heralded the way out—a green and clattering refuge that would catapult them into the cool blue sky far from the mosquitoes, leeches, and thirst, and the sudden, random, and always unexpected butchery of war.

The chopper landed hard on the LZ, the ramp dropping heavily into tall grass. The air crew, carrying stretchers, hustled down the ramp to help with the loading of the wounded. Dylan glanced at the two door gunners, molded to their .50 caliber machine guns, wearing flight suits and, even in the deepening twilight, sunglasses, as though they were being filmed for a movie.

"C'mon, men, get 'em on the chopper!" The young lieutenant with a blond crew cut and wearing a bandage on the left side of his neck waved his .45 frantically like a traffic cop at rush hour, knowing how vulnerable to attack they were at this critical time. "Move it! Move it! Move it!"

Dylan helped lift a boy of eighteen on a stretcher. Staring down at his bloodless face, twisted in pain, he remembered only that he came from west Texas and had joined the company two days earlier.

Clutching the sticky rear handles of the stretcher, Dylan lumbered up the ramp into the hot, grease-smelling interior of the medevac. A shadowy figure directed them to an open spot, they placed their burden gently down on the metal floor, then he was running back down the ramp, sucking hot air into his lungs.

Suddenly Dylan saw dozens of slim, black-clad figures rising from behind earthen dikes out in the rice paddies. The sun's last slanting rays transformed them into silhouettes cut by tin snips, their rifle barrels winking with white light as they waded toward him through the thigh-deep water.

Grabbing his M–16, Dylan dove for the cover of the tree line and lay flat behind a fallen tree. He slammed a fresh clip home, jerked the receiver back, chambering the first round, then sighted toward the enemy. Some were crumpling beneath the fire of the movie-star door gunners, but others quickly took their place. Too many of them, he thought as he pressed the trigger and felt the rifle's stock bumping reassuringly against his shoulder.

". . . Dylan, wake up."

"Hmmm . . ." Dylan lifted his head, propping on one elbow, then swung his legs over the edge of the couch. "Is it time for supper already?"

"It's time for something else."

Rubbing the sleep from his puffy eyes, Dylan mumbled, "What are you talking about?"

"Get dressed," Susan said, heading back toward the bedroom. "I'll get my overnight bag."

Dylan rubbed the back of his neck, rested his elbows on his knees, and stared at the smooth cypress planks of the floor. He felt as though his head were filled with cobwebs . . . then it hit him, almost like an audible click between his eyes. "The baby!"

"He's figured it out," Susan muttered, ambling down the hall.

Dylan leaped off the couch, shot past Susan, bumping her into the wall.

Whirling back around, he took her by the shoulders. "I'm sorry. You all right?"

"I'm fine." Susan placed her hand on the small of her back. "Now, settle down and get dressed."

"I'll get your overnight bag." Dylan whirled around and sped down the hall.

"Dylan!"

He stopped and turned toward his wife, a look of exasperation on his face. "What is it now?"

"I'll get the bag," Susan said slowly and calmly. "I have to add a few things to it."

"What do you want me to do?" Dylan's eyes lighted with an idea. "I know. I'll call my mother and let her know so she can get there on time."

Susan grabbed his arm as he started past her toward the kitchen. "I've already called her."

"Emile . . . and Emmaline?"

Susan nodded. "Emile's bringing a unit so he can use the lights and siren on the way to the hospital. They'll be here in about fifteen minutes."

"What do you want me to do, then?"

Susan shook her head slowly, giving him a patient smile. "Get dressed."

Dylan glanced down at his rumpled shirt and sweat pants. "Oh yeah. Guess I'd better get some clothes on, huh?"

"Great idea," Susan mumbled as she walked past him, turning into the bathroom.

"Susan . . ."

She turned around, a slight edge to her voice as she spoke, "What is it now?" Then she saw the look on his face, and her expression softened.

"I'm . . . I'm just excited, Susan, that's all. And maybe a little bit worried."

"I know." She smiled and kissed him on the cheek. "Now, get dressed."

"Uhhh. . . !" Susan lay on the backseat, her head cushioned in Emmaline's lap.

Dylan glanced back at his wife, feeling helpless and totally useless, wishing that he could somehow take his wife's pain into his own body.

"The contractions are coming every five minutes now." Emmaline sat directly behind Emile, looking at her watch. "How much longer till we get to the hospital?"

Emile slapped the microphone back in place on the radio. He threaded the Ford, its dome light whirling in the rainy dark, through the trucks and tractors hauling the last of the day's sugarcane harvest to the mill. "Twenty minutes at the outside. Fifteen if it wasn't grinding-season traffic."

"Dylan . . ." Susan's voice sounded faint, as though the pain had robbed her of her strength.

"I'm right here, sweetheart."

"Hold my hand."

Reaching over the backrest, Dylan took Susan's hand. It felt dry and slightly cool, like the hand of someone afflicted with an extended illness. "It won't be long now, Susan. Emile had them patch him through to the hospital. The doctor'll be waiting for us when we get there."

"Good," she gasped the word out. "I don't know how much longer—ohhh . . ."

"Easy, sugar." Emmaline stroked Susan's forehead, murmuring words of comfort and reassurance to her; soft, cooing sounds as she would have spoken to a sick child.

Dylan felt her squeeze hard on his hand with every contraction. They were lasting almost a minute now with only four or five minutes from the beginning of one to the beginning of another.

Leaning forward, Emmaline whispered in Emile's ear, "Hurry! She's getting awfully weak."

Emile nodded and pressed the accelerator, whipping past the last of the cane trucks.

Dylan stared out through the windshield, the wipers swishing away at the slow, steady November rain. The wind had almost died away, with only an occasional gust rocking the stalks of cane along the roadside as they slipped into and out of the glare of the headlights.

Muffling a cry, Susan gripped his hand tightly again. Dylan felt as though another hand, hard and cold and huge, clutched at his heart with an iron grip. He recalled that warm spring day in their little cottage on Camelia Street in Baton Rouge when

Susan had first told him of her pregnancy.

Next to the brick patio in the backyard, bees were lifting off the new clover, green and April tender. The sounds of children at play in the shade of City Park live oaks drifted like summer memories on the jasmine-scented air.

Then the weather turned around. A wind blew out of the south-west, scattering cotton-ball clouds before it like thistledown. The sky turned slate gray and filled with rain that drummed on the glass-topped table where he had been writing a poem for Susan. The lines on crum-pled sheets of paper grew sodden and as insubstantial as smoke—but he was writing again for the first time since her terrible injury.

Coming out of his reverie, Dylan retained a final image from that day that seemed so long ago. After finishing the poem, he had gazed out the bank of windows that faced their backyard. Three sparrows, their brown feathers darkened with rain, sat motionless in the lower limbs of a crepe myrtle.

"Five minutes and we'll be there," Emile announced as the Ford droned over the I–10 bridge down into Baton Rouge.

"Make it four," Emmaline chimed in from the backseat.

Dylan gazed at Susan's face, shadowed in the dim glow of the dashboard and the brighter shining of the bridge lights. Her eyes were shut, her lips thin and pale, the skin taut across her cheekbones. He gave her hand a reassuring squeeze, wishing that the whole ordeal was over, that their child was already kicking and crying in healthy protest at being dragged into the world on such a chill and rainy night.

But in his mind's eye Dylan saw himself in the hospital waiting room, staring at a wall clock with hands that seemed to have petrified since his arrival.

Dylan gazed out the rain-streaked window at the parking lot, almost empty now beneath the arc lights, reflecting in its wet, glistening surface eleven lonely looking cars and one bat-tered '50s vintage pickup. He turned around and looked at Emile, sitting on a vinyl and chrome couch, his head nodding as he fought against the sleep that was about to take him.

Then Dylan's eyes were drawn toward the clock. It seemed as though someone had replaced it with a picture of a clock; the same size and shape but with hands that didn't move. It would forever be ten minutes past three on this Thanksgiving morning in the year nineteen hundred and seventy.

Sitting down in a wooden chair near the window, Dylan watched Emile lose the battle with sleep as he slumped slowly to the side, his head coming to rest on Emmaline's big leather purse she had left on the couch.

Resting his elbows on his knees, Dylan felt useless and helpless, unable to give Susan any comfort, unable to ease any of the pain she was going through. Feeling as though a great weight was bearing down on him, he leaned forward, placing both hands over his face.

Dear God. Oh, dear God! Please take care of my wife! Please take the pain away and let her have this baby without any problems. Lord, you know Susan's been through enough already . . . most of it my fault. I've been such a lousy husband . . . but I'm trying to change that now. She'll be such a good mother for this baby . . . but you already know that. I don't deserve anything from you, but if you'll just keep Susan safe I'll . . . I'll do what? What can I do for you, God? What can I possibly do that would make any difference?

A clear image suddenly appeared in Dylan's mind: a Sunday school class from his childhood; the long, low table and miniature chairs; the color pictures of little children gathered around Jesus. He remembered their teacher reading the story of how Jesus had confronted the Pharisees in the Temple, calling them hypocrites. *That's me—a hypocrite, a phony! I can't do anything to help Susan, God. I just ask you to have mercy on her and to keep her safe.*

"You okay?"

Dylan rubbed his face with both hands, then looked at Emile, puffy-eyed and leaning slightly to starboard where he had roused himself from sleep. "Yeah, I'm fine. Just resting my eyes a little."

Emile stood up, stretched, and ran his fingers through his hair. "How about a cup of coffee?"

"I expect the cafeteria's closed. Besides, I don't want to leave now. We might hear something anytime." Dylan, propping his elbows on his knees, stared blankly down the hall in the direction of the delivery room.

Emile gave him the look of a man who had been through it all before. "There's always coffee around somewhere in a hospital. I'll check the nurses' station."

Dylan nodded, stood up stiffly, and walked back over to the window. The rain still beat steadily down on the parking lot. A man in a hooded black raincoat ran from the neon glare of a side entrance out to a pickup. Dylan could hear faintly through the glass the motor straining to turn over . . . then it caught and sputtered to life, white smoke billowing from the tailpipe. The truck rolled slowly backward out of the space and rattled across the blacktop, its tires leaving twin furrows in the glistening surface.

"Here you go." Emile handed Dylan a Styrofoam cup of steaming, dark coffee.

Staring into the cup, Dylan said, "This looks like the stuff they used to surface the parking lot."

"I doubt it," Emile replied, taking a careful sip. "It'd probably eat the tires right off the cars."

Dylan glanced back down the hall. "Maybe we ought to go check. See what's happening."

"Nothing."

"How do you know?"

"I had them check down at the nurses' station. They'll let us know as soon as there's any news." Emile stared out into the rainy night. "Besides, Emmaline and your mother are with her. She's in good hands."

Dylan walked over, sat down on the couch, and rubbed the back of his neck.

Emile made a face at his coffee cup, then set it down in a green metal trash can next to the wall. Joining Dylan on the couch, he said, "Try to get your mind off things for a while, son. Women have been having babies for a long, long time."

"Susan hasn't."

Emile grinned and said, "I guess it was a dumb thing to say, but your wife's a strong girl. She may look fragile and delicate, but I believe she's a lot stronger than you give her credit for."

"Why do you think that?"

"She's put up with you, for one thing. Gotta be pretty tough to handle something like that."

"I guess you're right," Dylan said and nodded. For reasons that escaped him, he suddenly saw an image of Susan the night they had met at a dance in the huge, open-sided circus tent on the parade ground of the Algiers Naval Station. He saw her again as clearly as he had on that night in late summer—solitary, remote, and achingly lovely.

Although he had begun to doubt its existence, morning finally came to Dylan St. John. He opened the door quietly and stepped into the room, as hushed and shadowy as a midnight sanctuary. Smoky, pewter-colored light seeped in through the partially opened venetian blinds. Susan lay on the high, narrow hospital bed, her eyes closed, her face pale amid the dark tangle of her hair.

Dylan walked quietly over to the bed and gazed down at his wife. He wondered what toll the hours of pain had taken on her already weakened body.

"I thought you'd never come." Susan's words were as soft as the faint light floating in the room.

"How'd you know it was me?"

The corners of Susan's mouth lifted in a rumor of a smile. "Oh, Dylan . . . it's you."

A puzzled expression flickered across his face. "Who'd you think was coming?"

Susan opened her eyes slowly. "I was kind of hoping for Paul Newman, but I guess you'll have to do."

Dylan noticed the dark smudges of weariness on the delicate skin beneath her eyes. "I can see having this baby hasn't bothered your sense of humor."

"Sit next to me."

Dylan sat down carefully on the edge of the bed. Taking her slim hand, still cool, but no longer feeling dry, he kissed it, then enveloped it with his own. "How're you feeling?"

"Like somebody ran over me with a cane harvester."

"You're acting kind of giddy, young lady," Dylan said through a grin. "You sure y'all weren't having a party back there?"

"I think they gave me something." Susan giggled. "But they took something away first." She rubbed her stomach gently with her free hand.

"Looks like you've dropped a few pounds."

"I can't say I recommend the weight-loss program around here, though." Susan slipped her hand free, reaching toward Dylan's cheek. "Give us a kiss."

"At your service." Dylan leaned over and kissed her softly on the cheek.

"You can do better than that."

Dylan gave his wife a tender kiss on the mouth. It was something he had never grown tired of even after years of marriage. He had occasionally wondered how such a simple physical act could affect him the way it did. It had never been so with anyone else. Then he had finally decided that some things were beyond his comprehension. Drawing back slowly, he felt the warmth of Susan's lips coursing through his blood.

"Much better," Susan sighed, her eyes closed again. "She's beautiful, isn't she?" Her voice had grown suddenly weaker as she began slipping away beneath the drug-induced darkness.

"What. . . ?"

"Our daughter, silly."

"Yes, she is."

Susan smiled contentedly. "With that white hair people might wonder if she's really ours."

"Guess my dad had some strong genes for the baby to have hair just like his."

"She's so lovely. . . ."

Dylan felt a final soft pressure from Susan's hand, then she fell down into sleep, her breathing soft and regular.

"She's a fine girl, Susan," Dylan whispered, but the words of the doctor forced themselves into the joy of the moment, a shadow falling across the miracle of a firstborn child: "*. . . intracranial hemorrhage . . . sometimes happens in difficult deliveries. Ruptured blood vessels caused bleeding into the brain tissue. Convulsions and vomiting started one hour and twenty minutes after birth. Some difficulty in breathing. Sometimes the bleeding stops of itself before serious complications develop and there are no permanent effects.*"

Dylan had summoned all his strength to ask the terrible question. *"What if it doesn't stop?"*

"*. . . child could die or residual damage may occur . . . mental retardation or cerebral palsy.*"

Dylan caressed the soft skin on the inside of Susan's wrist. *I'll tell her tomorrow . . . or the next day.*

"Dylan . . ."

The sound of his mother's voice brought him out of the nightmare of the doctor's pronouncement. He turned slowly toward the door. "Yes, ma'am."

In the anemic gray light, Helen's pale face still carried the shadows of the long night. Her eyes somehow looked as though they belonged to a much older person. "The doctor wants to speak with you."

8

WHAT A FRIEND

Clumps of water hyacinth, their purple and yellow blossoms fading and falling with the arrival of the first cold front, floated among the cypress knees. Spanish moss lifted and tossed in the morning breeze. Long, thin, rippling clouds gave the blue sky a washboard appearance.

Billie sat at a folding table on the plywood deck of the houseboat, made from scrap lumber and fifty-five-gallon oil drums welded together to form two long pontoons. Her jeans and tailored denim blouse were wrinkled; her auburn hair pillow rumpled and slightly oily. "How do you like your breakfast?"

"It's real good!" Laura buttoned the top button of her new red coat, then took a bite of buttered toast.

"Sorry I broke the egg yolks." Billie sipped her coffee from a chipped teacup. "I never was much good in the kitchen. We always had somebody to cook and clean for us, so Mama never got around to showing me."

Laura took a bite of the greasy, hardened egg yolk. "It's better than Caleb can do." She chewed, her blue eyes sparkling. "And Daddy don't even try."

"Doesn't."

"What?"

"Daddy *doesn't* even try."

113

"Okay," she said with a grin, her cheeks puffed with food. Swallowing, she said, "Daddy and Uncle Caleb got home real late last night . . . didn't they?"

Billie nodded. "I don't know what happened, but Caleb sure was upset about something."

Laura poked at her watery grits with her fork. She thought again of the little store in the mountains and the loud noise and her daddy's torn jacket . . . and the blood. "Did Uncle Caleb talk to you about . . . anything?"

"No . . . not much. He said something went wrong on the job and somebody got hurt. That's all." Billie nibbled a crust of toast, washing it down with coffee. "I never heard of anybody going out to the rigs to work and coming back the same day. I thought they always stayed at least a week."

"I'm glad you came to stay with us, Miss Billie."

"Me too." Billie reached across the table and smoothed Laura's hair with the palm of her hand. "Your hair sure looks pretty since we washed it and used some conditioner."

"It never looked this pretty since my mama—" Laura broke off the sentence and stared at her food.

"Maybe I can be your mama for a little while," Billie offered. "Not a real mama, of course. You only have one of those. More like a make-believe mama."

"I hope you stay with us forever and ever."

"I don't know if I can promise that, Laura Lee. Forever is a long, long time."

Laura stared at Billie, a puzzled frown on her face. "Did the spoon hurt your mouth?"

"Did what?" Billie smiled at the turnings of a child's mind that would bring forth such a question. "I don't have the faintest idea what you're talking about."

"Before you came to live with us, I heard Uncle Caleb say you were born with a silver spoon in your mouth."

"Oh, he did, did he?"

Chewing a bite of toast, Laura nodded her reply.

"It's just a way of saying that somebody was born to a family

114

with . . . with . . ." Billie found the words surprisingly hard to speak. She finally blurted out, "A lot of money."

"Your mama and daddy got a lot of money?"

The question made Billie feel awkward. "Yep, but it's really not that important."

"I don't have no money. Does that mean I'm not as good as you?"

"Certainly not!" Billie picked Laura up and sat her on her lap. "Why would you ask such a thing?"

Laura shrugged. "Daddy always says rich people think they're better than us."

"Well, they're not, so you just forget about things like that. You're as good as anybody."

Laura thought of the tall houses with wide front porches and lawns decorated with flowers and shrubbery that she had seen in New Orleans. "Do you live in a big house?"

Billie nodded. She gazed at the cypress trees rising against the blue sky, mirrored in the dark surface of the bayou. "But it's prettier out here."

"What does it look like?"

"It has big white columns and wrought iron grillwork, and the grounds have old, old trees." She kissed Laura on the cheek. "And there's a big swimming pool out back. I bet you'd have a good time in there."

"Me too." Laura's face brightened at the thought of splashing in the pool with Billie. Then a tiny crease formed between her eyes. "Why'd you come out here?" She glanced at the door leading into the houseboat. "I don't think this is a nice place at all."

"It's . . . it's so different. I've never lived anyplace like this before." She took a deep breath, letting it out slowly. "And I don't have anybody telling me what I can do and what I can't do . . . ordering me around all the time."

"You like Uncle Caleb?"

"Yes, I guess I do. That's part of it." Billie lifted Laura off her lap and stood up. "Hey, I've got an idea! Why don't we take the boat and go fishing . . . or maybe just ride around the swamp and look at things? It's such a pretty day!"

Laura glanced at the door again. "I don't know if Daddy would like that."

"Oh, fiddle-dee-dee."

"Why'd you say that?"

Billie tossed her head, her auburn hair splashed with golden highlights. Then she smiled. "It's from a movie about the old South. Something a girl said when she decided to do something that everybody else thought was wrong."

"Would you take me to see it sometime?"

"Maybe."

Laura looked at the bateau tied to the rail of the houseboat with a yellow nylon line swinging in the morning breeze, which dented the water. "You know how to make the boat go?"

"Certainly." Billie grabbed a cane pole resting on two sixteen-penny nails driven into the wall, then picked up a can of worms from a shelf next to the door. "C'mon. We'll paddle far enough away from the houseboat so the motor won't wake your daddy up when I start it."

"Daddy's gonna be mad."

"Oh hush!" Billie opened the gate in the railing and helped Laura down into the bateau. Then she untied the line, stepped in, and sat down at the back of the boat next to the outboard. "I left home 'cause I got tired of being ordered around. I'm certainly not gonna let it happen out here."

"You don't know my daddy."

Billie paddled quietly away from the houseboat toward the other side of the bayou. "I don't think I want to know him either. Now, you just quit worrying and let's have a good time."

A solitary hawk, riding the thermals, soared in lazy circles against the soft blue sky. Far below, a black man in a khaki shirt and sun-faded blue overalls plunged his shovel into a pile of dark earth and dumped it into the rectangular-shaped hole. Grasping the end of the handle with one hand, he leaned on his shovel, pulled a red handkerchief from his back pocket, and wiped the sheen of perspiration from his face. Then he returned to the *chunk, chunk, chunk* of the shovel's blade biting into the earth with a steady, rhythmic beat.

Dylan, the coat of his black suit draped across his knees, his gray tie loosened, squatted against the trunk of an ancient magnolia. Staring at the open grave, he heard the black man's pleasant baritone voice rise in song.

"What a friend we have in Jesus,
All our sins and griefs to bear!
What a privilege to carry
Everything to God in prayer!"

As Dylan listened to the words of the song, he remembered what a true and faithful friend Father Nick had been to him all those years ago when he had lost his father. No matter how busy the priest's schedule, he had always found time to spend with a lonely and sometimes angry thirteen-year-old boy.

"Can we find a friend so faithful
Who will all our sorrows share?"

"You ready to go?" Emile, his navy pinstripe suit giving him the appearance of a banker rather than the sheriff of a South Louisiana river town, held his hand out toward Dylan.

Dylan grabbed the hand and lifted himself up. "Yeah. Nothing I can do here."

As they walked among the tilting old tombstones, weathered and worn and weary looking, Emile said, "You see anybody who looked like he didn't belong here?"

Dylan shook his head.

"I guess whatever perverse reasons killers have for showing up at their victims' funerals, they aren't a part of this one's makeup," Emile went on, heading for the white Blazer parked in the shade of a gnarled old cedar at the edge of the graveyard.

When he reached the truck, Dylan stopped and looked back at the man in the faded overalls, bending to his work. His dark face seemed filled with light as he sang.

"In His arms He'll take and shield thee;
Thou will find a solace there."

Emile climbed in the Blazer and started the engine. He glanced at Dylan, still standing next to the passenger-side door. "You going with me?"

"Huh . . . oh yeah." Dylan got in and slammed the door. He stared out the window at the slowly diminishing mound of raw earth and listened to the tires crunching along the shell drive as they left the cemetery.

———————

"We've got to get these guys." The muscles bunched beneath the taut skin along Emile's jawline.

Dylan stared out the window at the slow curve of the bayou on his right. He was still lost in thought, picturing Father Nick sweating in a tattered *Holy Cross* T-shirt as he gave Dylan his after-school lesson on the tennis court. "We will."

"You know something I don't?"

"They're in the Basin. That's the only place left they could be hiding."

"Lots of places to lose yourself in there."

"Mr. Verrett can locate 'em if anyone can."

Emile snapped his fingers. "Muskrat? Maybe he could at that. He knows the Basin as well as anyone alive and he still does some trapping and fishing. He might have seen them already and just didn't know who they were." He glanced at Dylan. "You and Muskrat hit it off pretty good, didn't you?"

"Yep." After first meeting the old man who had spent his entire life hunting, trapping, and fishing in the Basin, Dylan found it difficult to call him by his long-time nickname, Muskrat. "I'm going to see him first thing in the morning. I'd go this afternoon," Dylan added, feeling as though he was shirking his duty, "but I'd better go check on Susan and the baby instead."

Glancing at his friend, Emile said, "That's *exactly* what you should do this afternoon." Then he added, "The fog can get pretty thick back in the Basin this time of year. Think you'll be able to find Muskrat's place without getting lost?"

"Yep. I'm getting better at finding my way through all those bayous and pipeline canals."

"I know you've got a personal interest in finding these guys, Dylan, but if you need time off to stay with Susan in the hospital, take all you need."

Dylan watched a snowy egret lift from the trunk of a fallen tree and sail above the smooth surface of the bayou. "We've already talked it over. She thinks I should go after the men who killed Father Nick. Since she won't be going home for a few more days anyway, she'll be at the hospital with Erin all the time."

"Erin St. John," Emile said. "Yes, sir, that's got a real pretty ring to it." He noticed the shadow crossing Dylan's face. "She's going to be all right, Dylan."

"I hope so." Dylan leaned his head downward, stretching the kinks out of his neck. "I was so worried about Susan, and now there's the baby. . . ." His voice became a whisper. "And there's nothing I can do for her."

"Sure there is."

Dylan turned toward Emile. "Even the doctor doesn't know . . . for sure. What can *I* do?"

"The same thing fathers have done since creation," Emile replied as though it should have already been perfectly obvious. "You can love her . . . and you can pray for her."

A light seemed to break through the cloud around Dylan. "I can do that much, can't I? And I can be at that hospital every day; be there with Susan . . . and our little girl." He looked at Emile as though for approval. "That's something I can do."

"That's something we all can do for the people we love. Just be with them, stay close, let them know they can depend on us no matter what happens. We can't make everything right in this ol' world, son," Emile said, swerving to avoid a nutria that scurried across the road and splashed into the bayou, "but that don't mean we have to roll over and play dead every time we get a hard knock or two either."

Suddenly Dylan felt as though a fog had begun lifting from his mind. He had been so burdened and confused by the events, the turmoil, the sorrow of the past days, that the world had seemed somehow unreal; a place where he was simply buffeted about by circumstances with no way to fight back. "And I'm going to hold up my end of this investigation too," he assured Emile. "You can count on that."

"Never had any doubts in the first place." Emile cleared his throat like someone stepping before a microphone at a banquet. "I just got some news that's probably going to complicate things on this case even more than they already are, but I'm afraid we're just going to have to put up with it."

Dylan gazed out the window at the autumn wild flowers, frost burned and sad looking, along the side of the road. "Well, let's have it."

"After Judge LeBlanc found out that his daughter ran off with one of the robbers, he used some political clout to call out the National Guard."

"That's all we need," Dylan moaned. "Did he give you any reason for it, or does he just want to show everybody what a big stick he carries?"

Shaking his head slowly, Emile replied, "The man's distraught about his daughter, and he's just trying anything that comes into his head to get her back."

"Did anybody think to give these boys a short course on law enforcement? Going on field maneuvers is a little different from arresting civilians." Dylan pictured a Cajun National Guard company blowing away the two armed robbers and everybody else within a one hundred-yard radius. "You don't end up being cross-examined in the witness box."

Emile smiled. "As bad as it sounds, we've got two things in our favor."

"Good," Dylan muttered, still staring out the window. "I'm about ready for some good news in this case."

"First of all, the governor only authorized a call-up of twenty men, and they're all from a local unit."

"Doesn't sound too bad so far." Dylan turned toward Emile. "What else?"

"It's hunting season."

"I know that much already," Dylan said. "But what does that have to do with anything?"

"Well," Emile smiled, "the 'good ol' boys' kicked up such a ruckus about missing a day in the woods that the governor only authorized one day."

Dylan took his tie off and stuffed it into his coat pocket. "Great. Now if the 'good ol' boys' in army green don't scare the bad guys off, we might have a good shot at finding them."

"Where's the boat?" Ryder stepped out onto the deck of the houseboat, squinting in the pale December sunlight. He wore an unbuttoned green fatigue shirt, a pair of dark blue work pants, and black wool socks.

Caleb took a pair of aviator sunglasses out of the pocket of his khaki shirt, shoved them on his face, and glanced at the railing where the bateau had been tied. "Guess the girls took it out for a spin." He tried to sound casual but couldn't quite manage to keep the nervous edge out of his voice.

Ryder's face contorted with sudden anger, his mouth a thin, pale slit. "Did you tell that rich brat she could go off with Laura in my boat?"

"No, Jack. Honest, I didn't!" Caleb had grown used to his brother's threats against him but now feared for Billie's safety. "What could it hurt if they take a little boat ride?"

"Are you nuts? What if she takes a mind to go on back to Mommy and Daddy?" He scowled at Caleb, then made a sweeping gesture with his arm. "Next thing you know this place is neck deep in cops."

"She's not going to do anything like that. We—we've got an understanding. Besides, she really likes Laura Lee. She's almost like a big sister to her, or a mother even."

Ryder grew sullen, his gaze turning inward as though staring back through the years at his long litany of defeats. "You got a lot to learn about women, kid." He stepped inside the houseboat, returning with a can of Jax beer.

"You gonna start drinking already?" Caleb leaned back on the railing made of welded pipe.

"Hey," Ryder replied with a grin, "I had a rough night. I'm off duty now so give it a break, will you?" He sat down in an aluminum folding chair painted green and took a hard pull from his can. "When you gonna be ready to hit another joint?"

"After that last one . . . maybe never."

Ryder gave him a sardonic grin. "What's the matter, you ain't man enough for this line of work?"

Anger surged through Caleb like an electric current, followed by regret that he had ever listened to his brother's promises of the easy life. "You think gunning down two unarmed men makes you a man, Jack?"

"They had it comin'!" Ryder gulped at his beer, then stood up, both fists doubled at his side. He stepped toward Caleb, then stopped, tilting his head to one side like a dog listening to a strange noise.

Caleb heard it too. The sound of an outboard, its whine getting steadily louder. Then he saw them: Billie, sitting in the stern of the bateau, running the motor; Laura, sitting on a boat cushion amidship, her face bright with laughter and excitement.

"Here comes your rich brat." Ryder gave his brother a sidelong glance. "I think it's about time that her and I had a, what did you call it, an *understanding.*"

"Why don't you leave them be, Jack? Look at your daughter. I haven't seen her this happy since . . ." Caleb let his words trail off without mentioning his brother's wife.

Billie steered the bateau in a looping curve, cutting the motor so it glided up to the side of the houseboat and bumped gently against the old tires hanging alongside. "You should have come with us, Caleb. We had the *best* time!"

Laura's blue eyes, crinkled almost shut with her smile, seconded Billie's comment.

"Git outta that boat!" Ryder reached down, grabbed Laura by the wrists, and snatched her from her seat in the bateau. Dropping her on the deck, he turned toward Billie. "And you . . . the next time you take off in that boat"—he glanced at Caleb—"or anywhere else, for that matter, you're gonna wish your snotty mama and daddy wouldn't of had no children!"

Billie stood up, the boat wobbling with her anger as she shouted, "Why don't you act like a daddy for once in your pitiful life and quit blaming that little girl for your troubles? She didn't make your wife run off, and she doesn't fill your gut full of alcohol every day!"

Holding tightly to the collar of Laura's coat, Ryder glowered at Billie, his dark eyes like buckshot in his florid face. Words seemed inadequate for the wrath building up inside him. He finally turned to Caleb. "You better talk to *that* one." His voice had lowered to a guttural snarl. "Next time she shoots her mouth off like that . . . something real bad's gonna happen!"

Billie looked toward Caleb as though asking for support in her tirade against Ryder. Caleb turned his eyes from her face, watched his brother hustle Laura through the door of the houseboat, then turned away and stared at the sunlight glittering on the wind-ruffled surface of the bayou.

———————

A bobcat, sharp-eared, tall, and lean in the flanks, stepped gingerly to the muddy shoreline, bordered by willows and cattails. Moonlight glimmering on the water lent the predator an insubstantial quality as though he had been molded from cobwebs. He lowered himself carefully on his front legs, surveyed both banks with practiced movements, and drank soundlessly, lifting his head every few seconds.

"Shhh . . ." Caleb put his finger to his lips, making a downward motion with his other hand as Billie opened the door and stepped out onto the deck.

"What's the—"

Caleb waved her into silence and motioned for her to join him at the railing. When she got there, he pointed across the bayou in the direction of the bobcat.

Billie peered out through the moon's pale, shimmering light toward the opposite bank. Then she saw it, her face opening in delight at the bobcat's phantom presence across the water. She grinned at Caleb, then looked back, but the big cat had vanished as though it had been a mere reflection floating in the shadowy dark at the edge of the forest.

"It's gone. . . ." Billie's voice took on a hushed, breathless quality as though the cat's disappearance had taken its place among a long succession of losses in her life.

Caleb nodded. "It's hard to believe it was really there. It was so . . . so delicate and graceful." He glanced back at the spot where the cat had drank from the bayou. "I've seen bears up in Tennessee but never a bobcat."

Billie stepped close to Caleb, letting her hand slip inside his. "You're certainly not like most boys I know."

"What's that supposed to mean?" he said. "Did I do something else wrong?"

"Don't be so defensive." Billie waved his doubts away with a flick of her wrist. "I just mean most boys would have been thinking about some way to shoot that beautiful creature." She leaned forward, kissing him on the cheek. "You only thought about what a lovely picture it made, taking a drink there in the moonlight next to the bayou."

Caleb felt a slight warmth rising up his neck and into his face. "Yeah, well, I guess I've done my share of shooting too." The words touched off a flash of memory: the roar of his brother's .357 in the confines of the old store and the spreading red splotches on the tan raincoat and the white apron.

"What's the matter, Caleb?" Billie touched his hand gently. "Did I say something wrong?"

Shaking his head, Caleb tried to push the memory out of his mind. "No. It's nothing you said. I just . . ." He put his hands on her shoulders. "You're not too cold out here?"

Billie slipped beneath his hands and placed her arms around his waist. "Not now."

Caleb held her and pressed his face against her soft hair. The fragrance reminded him of summer wild flowers he picked for his mother as a boy in the Tennessee mountains. "You're not sorry you came with me, are you?"

"No . . . I'm not. But your brother doesn't like me. Maybe I should leave."

Caleb stepped back, gazing into her upturned face. "Don't say that!" Surprisingly, he felt close to panic at the thought of being without Billie. After the concert he had dropped his tough-guy act with her and felt he could be himself for the first time since he could remember. "You're the best thing that's ever happened to me. I don't know what—"

"Shhh . . ." Billie placed her finger against his lips. "I'm not going to leave." She smoothed his hair along his temple with the backs of her fingers. "Not without you . . . and Laura Lee."

"I don't understand."

Billie's voice took on the urgent whisper of someone suspecting a prowler in a darkened house. "We've got to get away from Jack! The three of us."

"But he's my brother . . . the only family I've got left, except for Laura Lee. And I can't take her away from her father."

"She'd be better off dead than with that . . . that monster. She's scared to death of him."

"Don't talk like that. Jack's just going through a rough time. He's been hurt real bad."

"Not as bad as he hurts other people, especially Laura. We've got to get away from him."

Caleb knew Billie was speaking the truth about his brother even without knowing the terrible things he had done. He found himself giving way to the logic of her words, almost the same words he had spoken to himself for months. "You're right. We'll leave and take Laura with us."

"Oh, Caleb, I'm so happy!" Billie threw herself into his arms. "We'll be like a real family."

"But we can't do it right now."

Billie stepped back, her face slack with disappointment. "Why not?"

"We'll never get away with it if we just blunder into this thing. We've got to make plans."

Billie glanced at the door of the houseboat as though expecting Ryder to burst through it at any moment. "We'd better not take too long."

"Don't worry, we won't." Caleb felt a rush of fear and uncertainty. Then he looked at Billie and knew he would do whatever it took to keep her with him. He felt he had aged years in the past few minutes. The last bright vestiges of youth seemed to flicker and die in the passing of time's soundless wind.

"There's one thing your brother said that I agree with completely," she said.

"What's that?"

Billie gazed across the bayou at the forest, a wall of darkness buttressed against the vast, star-crowded dome of the sky. "Something bad's gonna happen."

9

ANGEL AND STONE

Wearing boots, Levi's, and a denim jacket over his heavy khaki shirt, Dylan killed the engine of the ten-horsepower Mercury outboard and let the bateau drift across the dark surface of the small lake. A curtain of fog hung over the water, crawled out onto the banks, and hung like strips of torn cotton in the lower limbs of the trees.

Directly ahead of Dylan, dead limbs, decaying leaves, and ragged black husks littered the ground beneath a hickory tree rising from the hammock of dry ground that Muskrat Verrett had chosen for his home. The underbrush had been cut away years before, leaving only the tall, widely spaced trees, their limbs and trunks wrapped and hung with thick vines.

Wreathed in mist, the clapboard shack stood between two ancient tupelo trees. White smoke curled from the chimney. Concrete block steps led up to a gallery that held two straight-backed chairs with deer-hide seats. A well-worn path led from the steps past the rosebushes and down through the frost-burned weeds to the lake.

As the bateau slid up onto the muddy bank next to a battered handmade pirogue, Dylan stepped out and pulled the flat-bottomed boat halfway out of the water. Reaching back into the boat, he grabbed a carton of Fleer's Double Bubble chewing gum and a thick new paperback, then headed up the path toward the cabin and the sound of a gasoline-powered generator's metallic stutter.

As Dylan stepped onto the front porch, he could hear a scratchy version of Gershwin's "Rhapsody in Blue" struggling to rise above the din of the generator. The mud-caked brogans next to the wall reminded him of his father's that had sat on the back porch of their home in Algiers. He knocked on the door. "It's Dylan St. John, Mr. Verrett."

A chair scraped across the floor, and the music ended with a *pop* as the phonograph needle was lifted from the record. The door swung inward, sunlight falling on Alton Verrett's narrow, seamed face, slim nose, and thick white hair. Wearing a red flannel shirt and threadbare overalls, he showed his amazingly white teeth. "Nobody but you calls me *Mr. Verrett*. Did you know that, young Dylan?"

"No, I didn't." Dylan felt his spirits rise with his first glimpse of Verrett's smile.

"The young people these days don't seem to have much respect for us old folks." He motioned for Dylan to come in and turned back into the dim interior of his home. "Maybe we don't deserve any. We've left you a legacy of war and racial hatred and . . ." His brief list seemed to collapse under its own weight. "As if enough of our youngsters weren't getting killed in Vietnam, now we shoot down four more at Kent State."

"I expect we don't have any worse problems than your generation did." Dylan followed Verrett across the smooth, bare wooden floor past a handmade table next to a curtainless window. Several shelves held a meager assortment of canned goods, sugar, flour, coffee, and other staples. The smell of woodsmoke mingled with that of old grease.

At a cast-iron stove in the far corner, Verrett sat down in one ladder-backed chair, offering the other to his guest. "Maybe not. But Americans used to stand together when trouble came. Now everybody's running off in different directions." He glanced at the box and the book in Dylan's lap. "Something went terribly wrong here around the time Kennedy was assassinated and . . ." Pushing at the air with the flat of his hands as though to dissipate his country's troubles, he said, "That's enough of that. You didn't come out here to listen to my dime store philosophy."

Even though they were two generations apart, Dylan found that he agreed with most of Verrett's opinions. "Here's a little Christmas gift for you in case I don't see you again for a while." He placed the book and carton of gum in Verrett's outstretched hands.

The old trapper grinned with his white teeth and faded brown eyes. "You've made an old man's day, son." He placed the gum on the floor next to his chair and hefted the heavy paperback. "*The New Yorker Book of Poems*. Ought to be one or two in here worth reading."

"I think so," Dylan agreed. "It's one of the best anthologies I've run across." He looked around the cabin at the shelves and stacks and boxes of books.

Verrett briefly thumbed through the book, then opened the carton, unwrapped a chunk of gum, and popped it into his mouth. "My only remaining vice," he mumbled as he chewed the gum with relish. "Now, I know you didn't come out here just to bring me greetings and gum. What's on your mind?"

Dylan gave him a rundown of the robberies, descriptions of the suspects, and other facts they had on the case. "I just thought you might have already run across them somewhere out in the Basin."

"Can't say as I have," Verrett muttered around the wad of bubble gum.

"There's a good possibility they may have Judge LeBlanc's daughter with them."

"Kidnapping?"

Dylan shook his head. "Not as far as we know. We think she met the younger man in town, got to be friends with him, and just took off."

"She's run off a time or two before, hasn't she?"

"How did you know about that?"

"I don't get into town but once or twice a month, but that's all it takes to catch up on Evangeline's goings-on."

"Mr. Verrett, I want you to be careful if you see these men," Dylan warned, part of him afraid that the old man *would* find them. "They're extremely dangerous, especially the older one. Just get word to us where they are."

Verrett's eyes crinkled with humor. "Don't fret yourself about that, young Dylan. I had enough guns pointed at me on the Western Front in 1918 to last me the rest of my life." He chewed thoughtfully. "If I find 'em, though, I'm coming straight to you. You get a whole mess of deputies chasing in after them and one of the girls just might not make it out alive."

"We can talk about that if you happen to find them." Dylan knew it would be a delicate balancing act to capture the two men and ensure the safety of the girls. "One more thing."

"Just one, now." Verrett's eyes lighted with new life. "Then we get down to some serious discussion of poetry. You've got to lead me through this new anthology." He picked up the paperback and placed it on his sparse lap. "Since you bought it for me, I assume you've read at least part of it."

"Yep."

"All right, then, let's get the official business over with."

"The governor's activated a local National Guard unit to search the Basin for his daughter. But," Dylan rushed to assuage the disappointment he saw crawling across Verrett's face, "it's only for one day."

"They're not issuing them live ammunition . . . surely."

"I'm afraid so. The girl's almost certain to still be with the men who committed murder and armed robbery."

"Oh no!" Verrett gave Dylan a look of mild desolation. "There won't be a thing that swims, flies, runs, or slithers left alive in the whole Basin."

"I'm sure it won't be that bad."

"I've seen them on maneuvers out here in the swamps before." Verrett's face looked as though he was reliving part of his time in the trenches of World War I. "You get that bunch of welders and pipefitters and oil field workers together, then you add some automatic weapons and a few cases of beer . . ." He let his words trail off as though his vocabulary couldn't handle the results of the recipe he had just concocted.

"Beer? They're not going to be drinking beer."

A touch of disbelief flickered in Verrett's eyes. "And nobody smoked dope over in Vietnam either." A slightly crooked smile ran across his face. "You turn that crew of Cajuns loose in these swamps and they'll be cracking the beer cans open before the sun clears the treetops."

"Nothing I can do about it," Dylan admitted.

"When they coming?"

"Saturday."

Verrett nodded his head slowly. "Reckon I'll just spend the day underneath my bed." Then he laughed and opened the book to the table of contents. "Now, what's a good poem to start with?"

"Susan had the baby."

Verrett looked stunned, then surprised, and finally joyful. "Why, that's wonderful, young Dylan! Just splendid. What is it, boy or girl?"

"A little girl. Erin," Dylan said with a hint of disbelief in his voice. He still found it difficult, even after seeing his daughter, to believe that he was truly a father.

"That's a pretty name. Susan's fine, I suppose."

"A little tired."

"Well, I'm just so happy for both of you. And what do you think of the miracle of birth?"

Dylan smiled weakly. "I think I'm still in shock. It really hasn't registered yet."

"Guess it's worth a trip to town, bad as I hate civilization, to see this miracle child."

"We'll look forward to it." Dylan found that he couldn't tell Verrett about his daughter's medical problems. It seemed to him that the telling of the trouble somehow made it more real and made the three of them more vulnerable.

"Now"—he glanced down at the book in his lap—"this looks interesting. Howard Nemerov's *Angel and Stone*."

Dylan walked along the waxed and gleaming floor in the late-night hush and antiseptic smell of the corridor. Easing the door open at Susan's room, he saw the empty bed and her opened Bible on the nightstand amid the hospital clutter. He knew where she would be, the place she had spent most of her days and much of the weary, endless nights.

Approaching the Neonatal ICU, Dylan saw Susan through the glass wall, sitting in a plastic chair next to one of several incubators arranged in abbreviated rows. Just beyond her, a gowned and gloved nurse, her arms shoved through rubber portholes, counted a child's apical pulse with a stethoscope.

Dylan stopped in the tiny anteroom, donned a white gown and surgical mask, then entered the main unit into the low hum and rush of air, the beeps and bleeps of monitoring equipment, the gurgling of oxygen bottles, and the weak, muffled cries of the babies.

Stopping behind Susan, Dylan placed his hands on her shoulders, leaned over, and kissed her on the cheek. "How's it going, sweetheart?"

Susan took his hand as he walked around next to the incubator. "Not much change." She glanced at their sleeping daughter. "She frets once in a while," she said, then hastened to add, "but not very much. She's such a good baby."

Dylan squatted next to his wife, staring at the child; the pink skin, perfectly formed features, and the silky, pale gleaming of the white-blond hair. "She certainly doesn't look like there's anything wrong with her."

Susan smiled weakly. "That's what I keep thinking. She's so precious . . . and such a *good* baby." She looked hopefully into her husband's face. "The doctor said the bleeding could stop by itself at any time . . . and there'd be no complications."

"She's going to be just fine," Dylan said, trying to put as

much conviction as possible into his words.

"I can't wait to get her home in her own room. Just think how much fun it'll be to hold her every day and feed her and . . ." Susan's words ended in a fading whisper.

Dylan gazed at his wife. Her weakened condition and the long nights with little sleep had given her green eyes a dull, glazed appearance. The delicate skin beneath them held dark blurs of weariness. Her hair, pulled back severely from her face and tied with a white ribbon, looked dull and drab. These things registered in Dylan's mind, but his heart told him that Susan was still the most desirable woman he had ever seen. "Why don't you go get some rest, Susan. I'll stay with Erin."

"Maybe in a little while." She reached inside the incubator through the portholes and lightly stroked Erin's hand—soft, delicate, and heartbreakingly tiny. "You making any headway in finding those robbers . . . and murderers?"

"Not a whole lot. I went to see Mr. Verrett today. He's going to see if he can locate them." Dylan watched the nurse whisper past them on the opposite aisle. "He travels all over the Basin fishing and trapping or just trying to find places he's never seen before. It's a different kind of life he's living."

"You really like him, don't you?"

Dylan nodded. "If it wasn't for you"—he glanced at the sleeping child—"and Erin, I might just move out there with him . . . somewhere in the Basin."

"We're pretty close right now."

"Yes, I know," Dylan agreed, "and I wouldn't trade places with anybody." He gave Susan's free hand a reassuring squeeze. "It's just that after what happened to Nick . . . well, there doesn't seem to be anyplace in the world where people are safe." Placing his other hand over Susan's, he continued. "I never really thought about it much until you came along"—he glanced through the incubator's protective glass—"and then we had Erin."

"The three of us are going to be fine," Susan said, her voice tinged with a weary sadness just beneath the confidence of her words. "As soon as Erin gets past this . . . this little problem and we get back to our home."

Dylan leaned forward and placed his lips gently on hers, lingering in the sweet warmth of their kiss. Drawing away, he whispered, "Why don't you go get some rest and let me get better acquainted with my daughter?"

"I'll make a deal with you."

"Okay, what is it?"

"You had supper yet?"

Dylan had to think about it. "No, I guess I haven't stopped long enough yet."

"I didn't think so," Susan said, pushing her hair back from her eyes. "You go and get a bite of supper. When you get back, I'll let you take over for me."

"The cafeteria's closed, isn't it?"

Susan glanced at the big schoolhouse clock on the wall. "I believe it is. You can go down to Jesse's place. I'll bet you haven't been there since we moved to Evangeline."

"You're right. I'd almost forgotten about the man who makes the best hamburgers in town."

"It's settled, then. You go see Jesse and I'll sit right here and watch Erin get well."

Standing up, Dylan gave his daughter a final long look, then kissed Susan and walked past the row of incubators striving to keep life flowing through their tiny occupants. At the main lobby, he opened the door just in time to see the first heavy drops splatter onto the lighted walkway leading down to the parking lot. Then a chill wind gusted out of the northwest, moaning around the angles and hollows of the building's stone walls, and the rain came pelting down in earnest.

Dylan stood in the cold spray blowing in under the high porte-cochere. *Perfect timing, Dylan.* He gazed out beyond the glistening parking lot and dark, rain-pocked surface of the lake. Four hundred feet in the air a cross glowed against the lime-stone facade of the capitol building. Created by employees who leave their office lights on one month each year, it celebrated a birth. He thought of the birth of *his* only child . . . and of what her life might be like.

———————

Wiping the counter and listening to Louis Armstrong's brass trumpet and gravelly voice on the jukebox, Jesse wore a stiff white apron that was almost the color of his close-cropped hair. His walnut-colored skin shone beneath the neon. The sound of the bell over the door drew his attention from his work. "Dylan St. John. I thought you'd died and gone to New Orleans."

Dylan smiled at his old friend. "Not quite, but I went to New Orleans and almost died."

"You did what?"

"Nothing. Just trying to make a joke that turned out to be unfunny." The words had seemed to come directly from some unconscious level before Dylan realized he had spoken them. He had tried to put his recent experience behind him but realized that it still lurked just beneath the surface, and sometimes a clawed and scaled limb would poke through.

Leaning on the counter with both hands, Jesse studied Dylan's eyes. "It's more than a joke, St. John. If you ask me, somebody ripped a hunk out of your soul."

Dylan leaped away from the subject. "Only thing I'm asking you is whether you got time to fix me a hamburger."

Jesse glanced around the empty cafe. "I might kin jes' work you in somehow."

Smiling, Dylan plopped down on one of the red-cushioned chrome stools. "Lots of grilled onions, Jesse."

"I fixed you 'bout a thousand hamburgers. I reckon I know how you like 'em."

Dylan watched Jesse preparing the food, his lean body working in a perfect economy of motion. It reminded him of a character from an E.A. Robinson poem. Jesse was by no means "clean favored" like Richard Cory, but he was "imperially slim."

"Guess who dropped by to see me the other night?" Jesse offered, turning the thick, homemade hamburger patty over on the grill that looked about the same age as the man using it.

"Beats me." Dylan scanned the front page of a *Morning Advocate* left on an adjacent stool. "Dianna Ross and the Supremes, maybe?"

Jesse ignored Dylan's second failed attempt at humor. "That Jacobs boy. You know, the one who got hisself in all that trouble about a year ago."

"Ike? No kidding?" Dylan folded the newspaper and set it aside. "What's he up to these days?"

"Told me he was working for the FBI."

Stunned, Dylan thought back to the past year when he had gone to visit Ike in the downtown jail. "Is he living across the river with his granddaddy?"

Shoveling the sizzling hamburger patty off the grill, Jesse dumped it onto a fresh bun. "Not anymore. Said he moved back over here a couple of months ago."

"Did he say where?"

"Yeah, I believe he did." Jesse gazed thoughtfully at the hamburger as he added the grilled onions, fresh tomato slices, and chopped lettuce. "Now I remember! He's got a place in that apartment building over by Capitol Lake."

"The one closest to the interstate?"

Jesse slapped mayonnaise and mustard on Dylan's hamburger, dropped it onto a heavy white plate, and set it in front of him along with a glass of water. "That's the one." Fishing in his pocket, he pulled out a quarter and headed for the jukebox.

"You didn't happen to get the apartment number, did you?" Dylan added Tabasco to his burger, then took a big bite, savoring the hot, juicy meat, fresh vegetables, and the spicy-hot seasoning.

"I wudn't doin' no police report on the man, St. John." Jesse punched at the jukebox buttons, then returned to his post behind the counter.

Dylan chewed contentedly, watching Jesse attend to sweep-

ing, dishwashing, and other cafe duties. Behind him the jukebox spilled over with the elegantly smooth and polished voice
of Nat King Cole singing "Stardust."

"How're you and Susan getting along these days?" Jesse
asked, wiping his hands on the front of his apron.

"We've got a little girl, Jesse."

"Git on away from here." Jesse's whole face crinkled in a
grin. "You don't mean it."

"I do."

"How old is she?"

"Two—" Dylan glanced at a Barq's Root Beer clock near
the jukebox—"almost three days now."

"I bet she's pretty like her mama, ain't she?"

Dylan nodded, then felt the grief and worry brimming
deep in his chest. "She's . . . she's got some health problems.
Probably going to have to stay in the hospital for a while."

Jesse's eyes gazed out beyond the rain-streaked windows,
then he said, "We ain't got no promises in this ol' world about
the folks we love." His voice carried undertones of old griefs
and whispered sorrows. "All we can do is enjoy them while
they're with us and love 'em as much as we can."

Dylan pondered the words that he would have never expected to come from Jesse. The same record began to play again
on the jukebox. *There's got to be more.* Finished with his meal,
he stood up and gave Jesse a farewell handshake. He stepped
out into the slow December rain as Nat King Cole sang:
"When our love was new and each kiss an inspiration . . ."

––––––––––

Turning slowly into the parking lot, Dylan listened to the
blue Volkswagen's tires crunching across the gravel as he parked
beneath a red oak. He got out and gazed at the four-story brick
building. It stood next to a finger of the lake southwest of the
Capitol building and across from the hospital where his infant
child lay in her glass womb. Traffic droned on the interstate as
he walked beneath the dripping trees toward the lighted en-

tranceway, then climbed the stairs.

"I must be having a dream," Ike said, standing inside the doorway in his sweat pants and *Southern Jaguars* T-shirt. Short and stocky, he had a modest Afro haircut and skin the color of café au lait. "Or maybe it's a nightmare."

"Glad to see you, too, Ike."

"C'mon in." He turned and walked across the bare wood floor and plopped down on a brown leather sofa. Glancing at his watch, he said, "You never were one for keeping civilized hours. You still playing the wounded poet role too?"

Sitting down in a matching leather chair, Dylan laughed. "No, I gave it up about the same time you dumped your political aspirations."

"I think it's more accurate to say they dumped me." Ike grinned. "But that's another story that you already know all too well."

"There's one thing I didn't know."

"Yeah, what's that?"

"That the FBI was hiring street thugs these days."

Ike started to reply, then his mouth wrinkled, laughter spilling out in a rush. Running both hands through his hair, he said, "I'm a lawyer, remember? I think that puts me about two notches below the street thugs."

"I guess you don't really qualify anyway," Dylan said matter-of-factly, "since you only spent one night in jail."

Leaning forward, arms resting on his knees, Ike said in a level tone, "You remember those two agents that came to interview me in the downtown jail?"

Dylan nodded. Through the open slats of the venetian blinds, he could see the lighted bulk of the hospital on the high point of land rising up from the lakeshore.

"Well, they saw right though that frame-up of Ralph's . . . and the 'powers that be' backing him." He rubbed a few remaining traces of sleep from his face. "Strangely enough, they hired me precisely because of the predicament I was in."

"I don't quite follow."

"They found out real quick that the heavy hitters made me the scapegoat for the whole rotten mess," he explained as though still slightly in awe of what had happened to him.

"And . . ."

"And who better to investigate political corruption in this state than somebody who's seen it from the inside?"

Dylan had begun to believe that maybe there was still some justice left in the world. "Are you telling me the FBI's got you handling political corruption cases now?"

Ike shrugged. "And I bet you thought there was no justice left in the world, didn't you?"

"Sounds too easy."

"There was a little more to it than that," Ike admitted, glancing out at headlights flickering by on the interstate. "I think the bureau checked out everybody that ever knew me from my first-grade teacher to the guy who cuts my hair." He suppressed a yawn with the back of his hand. "Now, St. John, tell me what's been going on with you and Susan."

Dylan brought him up-to-date on his life, including the birth of their daughter but excluding her medical problems. "And I need a favor from you, Ike."

"Imagine that! And here I am thinking you just dropped by for a midnight chat."

The abbreviated saga of the Basin-area armed robberies took fifteen minutes. "One of the witnesses said the camper had out-of-state license plates."

"If they've pulled any bank robberies, kidnappings, anything that would involve federal offenses, we might have a file on them?"

Dylan shrugged. "All we know for sure is the robberies and the two murders all look like the same two." He stared thoughtfully out at the lake. "I guess it's possible that the daddy could have taken his little girl without the mother's knowing, but I can't tell you anything for certain. Think you can find out anything for me?"

"If I can tie him in to a criminal or military record, I'll give you everything from his favorite color to his shoe size."

"A picture would be nice."

A ripple of concern passed over Ike's face. "The priest that was shot in the store in Breaux Bridge . . ."

"Yeah, it was him," Dylan admitted, surprised that Ike had remembered. "Father Nick was a good friend to me during a time when I really needed one."

"Tell you what. Send me a complete report over the teletype first thing in the morning, and I'll have one of the secretaries run a profile on these guys. It's amazing what the computer boys can come up with these days with just a little bit of information."

Dylan got up to leave. "I really appreciate this, Ike."

"Nothing to it." He followed Dylan to the door. "I thought I had some friends till I got in trouble. You were the only one to come see me when I was in jail."

10

SEVENTH CAVALRY

Perched in the crown of a leafless sycamore, a solitary crow sent his raucous call ringing out over the wetlands. Far below, two men dressed in army green chugged along the bayou in a fiberglass bass boat powered by a seventy-five-horsepower Evinrude.

Hearing the crow's faint call above the sound of the idling engine, Muley, who looked like a beer keg wearing a fatigue cap, tapped his friend on the shoulder. "Hey, Lester!" He pointed upward through the web of bare limbs toward the bird silhouetted against the blue sky.

Lester pulled back on the throttle lever, letting the backwash of the boat carry them toward the bank. Slim as a stiletto with a face almost as sharp, he said, "I hate dem crow, me. Dey give my garden fits every summer." Shoving his can of Dixie beer in a swivel holder screwed into the boat's dashboard, he grabbed his M–16 from the backseat and flicked the safety down to full automatic.

Muley joined Lester in his attack on the crow. Bursts of automatic fire shattered the stillness of the morning as well as a substantial part of the sycamore tree. Bits and pieces of limbs and bark showered down on the forest floor, the surface of the bayou, and the deck and interior of the boat.

Brushing wood chips from his face, Lester squinted upward

through the limbs. "I bet he don't go pecking at nobody's to-matoes no more, him." Then he saw the crow peer down at him briefly before sailing out over the treetops.

"Must be somet'ing wrong wit dis gun," Muley said, glaring at his M–16 as though it had betrayed him.

Lester snatched his beer from its holder, drained the can, and flung it out into the middle of the bayou. "I bet dis can don't fly away." Shouldering his rifle again, he emptied his clip toward the can, kicking up a spray of water. Then he scowled at the can wobbling in the small waves kicked up by the hail of bullets.

"Told you."

"Yeah," Lester agreed, tossing his rifle back on the seat. "Dey don't make nuttin' good as dey used to." Reaching into the ice chest at his feet, he pulled two cans of beer out, popped the tops off, and handed one to Muley. "I tell you one t'ing."

"I can't wait to hear dis, me." Muley grinned, turning his beer can up.

Lester gazed at the winter trees, the bayou, and the sky with its light covering of lacy white clouds. "Dis sho' beats hanging around dat smelly ol' armory on our regular weekend drills. Plus I git twenty-five dollars for using my boat."

"You can say dat again."

"Dis sho' beats hanging—"

"I know what you said," Muley cut him off. "You ain't got to tell me more den one time." He slouched down, resting his head on the back of the seat. "You reckon we got any chance at all of finding dem fellas who killed the priest?"

"I don't know, me. How we gonna find somebody we don't even know what dey look like?"

"We got a picture of de girl."

"A judge's daughter," Lester said, shaking his head in dismay. "I don't know what's wrong wit' people nowadays. Dis country's been goin' to de dogs ever since dat long-haired bunch from England come over here."

"The Beatles?"

"Yeah, dat's dem." Lester nodded mournfully, gulping down half of his beer. "Kids smoking dope and taking LSD, and women burning bras and hippies burning draft cards, and people wearing dem stupid Nehru jackets and bell-bottoms."

"And de music," Muley added woefully, "if you could even call it music. Dat stuff sounds like two wildcats fightin' in a room full of tin cans."

"I don't know, son. I just don't know." Lester finished his beer. "De worst was when we got back from Vietnam and dem people out in California spit on us and called us 'baby killers.' "

Staring at the sky, Muley listened to his friend's sad litany of social ills. "It's a mess all right."

"Guess we better get movin'. Ain't gonna find nobody sittin' around here all day."

Muley sat upright and took a swallow from his can. "What we gonna do if we do run across dem men?"

"Shoot 'em," Lester mumbled with no hesitation. He switched the ignition on and punched the starter button. The motor came to life with a rumble and the bubbling of its exhaust. "What else you do wid somebody who killed a priest?"

When he heard the automatic weapons fire, Ryder pulled the curtain back and peered out the window, then stepped out onto the deck of the houseboat. Gazing down the bayou in the direction the gunfire had come from, he saw nothing all the way to the point where the bayou curved sharply to the right. *What a time for Caleb to leave! Just when I might need him, he takes those girls off for a stupid boat ride.*

Just then the bass boat, bouncing crazily across the water, roared into sight around the curve. Ryder saw the two uniformed men, the driver waving his fatigue cap in the air like a cowboy astride a bucking horse, and heard a rebel yell ringing across the water. "Yeeeehaaaaaw!"

When the boat straightened out and headed directly at the houseboat, Ryder calmly stepped inside and grabbed the .45 automatic from a shelf. Checking the clip, he saw it was full, jammed it back in the pistol's handle, and flicked the receiver. Then he took a twenty-shot clip for his AK–47, filled it quickly and efficiently, shoved it into the bottom of the rifle, and snicked a round into the chamber.

Slipping the .45 inside his belt beneath his shirt, he grabbed the assault rifle and leaned it against the wall just inside the door. From outside, he heard the sound of the engine throttling down.

"Hey, anybody home in there?"

Pulling the curtain aside just enough to peer out, Ryder saw the man on the passenger side standing up, holding on to the top of the windshield for balance.

"What you t'ink, Lester?"

"Let's get out and take a look around." He killed the engine and let the boat glide toward the houseboat's tire bumpers hanging along the side.

Muley looked doubtful. "This is somebody's private property. We'd be trespassing?"

"We on official business, ain't we?"

"I guess you right." Muley tied the bowline to the railing and stepped onto the houseboat.

Ryder stepped through the door onto the deck, yawning and rubbing his eyes. Squinting into the sunshine, he asked, "What's going on out here?"

Lester reached behind him, grabbed his M–16, and placed it on the seat beside him. "We from the National Guard. The governor got us on special duty today."

"Oh *yeah*," Ryder said and grinned. "Sounds as official as all git-out. What's he got y'all doin', policing up cigarette butts out here in the swamps?"

Muley chuckled, letting the tension go out of his body, then glanced back at Lester.

In the company of a stranger now, Lester purposely shied away from his normal Cajun accent. "We looking for two men who killed a priest and a storekeeper." A slight frown spread across his narrow, dark face. "Sounds like you mighta spent some time in the service . . . either that or the jailhouse."

"You got that right." Ryder felt the reassuring, cold weight of the .45 pressing against his stomach. "A whole lot more time than I wanted to, that's for sure."

Lester began easing the M–16's safety down to the semiautomatic position. "You ain't telling us much about yourself, mister. You a jailbird or a grunt?"

Ryder noticed Lester's bony forefinger resting on the rifle's trigger guard. He calculated the time it would take him to undo the one button holding his flannel shirt over the .45, then snatch it from his belt and get off two or three rounds at each man. *I could take the fat one easy . . . but the skinny one's probably quick as a snake.* "You want me to go through the manual of arms with one of them M–16s," he asked, still looking for an opening, "or recite a few articles from the UCMJ?"

"He's been in, all right," Muley chuckled.

Lester's black eyes flicked over Ryder and took in as much of the houseboat as he could see. "What branch?"

"Army."

Muley nodded at Ryder's reply. "You didn't make it over to 'The Nam,' did you?"

Ryder gave Muley a benign smile. "Seventh Cav; the Ia Drang Valley; November 1965."

Lester's forefinger eased away from the rifle's trigger. "I be dog! If that don't beat all!"

"Don't tell me you know it." Ryder didn't miss Lester's movement and noticed that the cloud of suspicion seemed to be lifting from his face. He thought that the odds were now slowly swinging in his direction.

"Do we know it! We was both over there!" Muley broke in before Lester could reply.

Lester frowned at his excitable friend. "Settle down, Muley. We ain't time to take a trip down memory lane, no. You forgit we got business here?"

Ryder tried to steer them away from their "business." "November 1965. That's when the first real air-mobile operation in the whole Vietnam War took place."

"Where was you?"

"LZ X-ray."

Lester visibly relaxed, taking his hand off his weapon and using it to open the ice chest at his feet. "We was at LZ-Albany," he mumbled, reaching into the crushed ice and pulling out a beer. Holding it toward Ryder, he said, "Want one?"

"Don't mind if I do." Ryder caught the tossed beer one-handed and cracked the pull tab.

"What you doin' out here in the Basin?" Muley asked. "You don't sound like you from around here, no."

"You mean I don't sound like a Cajun even a little bit?" Ryder turned the can up and drained half of it.

"No, but you drink like a Cajun."

Ryder laughed and finished the rest of his beer. "That's not a bad way to wake up."

Taking two beers in one hand and slipping the other through the carrying handle of his M–16, Lester stood up and stepped from the gunwale of his boat to the houseboat's deck with feline agility. "You ain't answered my buddy's question, friend," he said, his eyes holding Ryder's. "Couldn't be that you trying to hide something, could it?"

"You don't have to bring that weapon on board my houseboat, do you?"

Lester's eyes narrowed. "Jist part of the job, partner. Don't go gettin' nervous on me, now." He tossed a beer to Muley, then drank from his own. "You still ain't answered the question. Maybe we ought to take a look around."

Ryder watched Lester take a long pull from his beer, then place it carefully on the table. "Me and the wife," he began, hoping to break the mounting tension that hung in the air like invisible storm clouds, "decided to take a little trip and ended up down here in Louisiana. We liked the cookin' "— he hoped to inject a feeling of casual camaraderie into the conversation—"and the people so much we decided to stay awhile."

"Why you out here in the middle of nowhere?"

"Look around you." Ryder made a sweeping gesture with his hand. "You ever see anything so pretty?"

"You might make a pretty good Cajun, you stay down here long enough." Muley grinned.

Lester was not so easily distracted. "Your wife wouldn't be about sixteen with pretty auburn hair, would she?"

Trying to keep the tension out of his voice, Ryder grinned. "I wish she was sixteen agin." He thought briefly of his run-away wife. "Wanda's almost thirty, and her hair's so blond you'd think it came out of a bottle, but it didn't."

"You don't have a little girl about five years old with blond hair, do you?" Lester asked, glancing at a scrap of paper he took from his top pocket.

"Nope. No kids."

"Why don't you ask your wife to come out here so we can take a look at her?"

Muley walked over from the railing and placed his hand on Lester's shoulder. "Why you givin' this boy a hard time, Les? He was in the Seventh Cav. We all went though the—"

Silencing his friend with a scowl, Lester turned back to Ryder. "You don't mind if we say hello to your wife, do you, partner? Now that we're ol' army buddies."

"She was in the bathroom a minute ago," Ryder said with a frown. "I'll take a look."

"We ain't going nowhere," Lester said, rubbing an oil-grained thumb along the trigger guard of the rifle as he spoke.

Ryder turned and went through the doorway. Inside, he knocked on an interior wall. "You still in there, baby?" Then he walked heavily toward the back of the houseboat, paused a few seconds, and headed quietly back toward the door leading out onto the deck.

Through the screened doorway, he saw the two men looking across the water, talking in low voices, their backs to him. He knew that even if they turned around, he was hidden from their sight in the shadowy interior of the houseboat. Stepping closer, he slipped the .45 from his belt, holding it with both hands, arms extended as he had been taught in advanced infantry training, and lined the sights up on the center of Lester's narrow back.

Somebody's bound to come looking for them tomorrow at the latest. One more try, then I finish them both. With a muffled curse, Ryder slipped the pistol back beneath his belt, grabbed a full bottle of sour mash whiskey from the cabinet and three plastic cups from the kitchen table, and stepped outside.

Lester turned around. "She comin'?"

"Wanda's asleep."

"Wake her up, then."

"I hate to do that," Ryder said, letting a slight whine creep into his voice. "She's been feeling poorly for the past couple of days. She really needs the rest."

Lester opened his mouth to speak, but Ryder interrupted him. "Look what I found, though." He placed the three glasses on the table, pulled the cork on the bottle, and poured liberally. "Have a snort. This stuff'll put hair on your chest."

Muley stared at the whiskey, gleaming with the sunlight's amber fire. His mouth hung open loosely. "Couldn't hurt nothin', right, Lester?"

A spark of protest flared in Lester's eyes, but the whiskey quickly doused it. "One drink," he said, "then we got to wake up your wife and take a look around."

Forty-five minutes later, Muley lifted the half-full bottle and poured four inches of whiskey into his plastic glass. "There ain't nothin' like swappin' tales with ol' army bubbies," he said, his eyes shining with alcohol.

"He's already your ol' bub"—Lester licked his lips, then concentrated on forming the word correctly—"bud-buddy. You jes met him an hour ago."

"He's still my good bubby."

"Right, Muley," Ryder chimed in, slapping the squatty little man on the back. "If we'd had a few more like you over in Nam, them skinny little boys in the black pajamas wouldn'ta had a chance." He sipped at the remaining ounce of whiskey left from the first and only glass he had poured for himself.

Lester pried himself out of his chair, standing unsteadily, his hand on the edge of the table for balance. "Whew! I gotta down a couple of beers so I can see straight agin."

"What you gittin' up for, you?" Muley seemed appalled that his friend would want to leave such good fun. He pointed with a weaving arm. "We got plenty lef' in dat bottle, yeah."

"We can't drink all de man's whiskey," Lester said. "Besides, we got more work to do. Let's check out dis houseboat and git on down de bayou."

Ryder knew he had them now but hoped to avoid any bloodshed that would only bring more guardsmen or law enforcement looking for them. "My wife's been real sick, Lester, and she's still sleeping. I'd hate to wake her up."

"Yeah, Lester," Muley chimed in, "we can't be barging in on no sick woman. Especially an ol' army bubby's wife. He went through the same hell over in Nam that we did."

Lester's expression grew morose, then his voice slipped down into a maudlin drone. "You right for once in yo' life, Muley. Ryder here," he lay his arm across Ryder's shoulders, "is as good as they come. Ain't no way he'd hurt nobody. We seen enough shootin' and killin' in our time, ain't we?"

149

"Right," Ryder agreed quickly.

"Let's go find dem robbers, den." Muley stood up and downed the last of his whiskey.

"Here, take the rest of it with you," Ryder said, offering the bottle to Lester.

Lester began shaking his head slowly. "Naw, we can't take a man's last—"

"Yeah, you can," Ryder cut him off, then shoved the bottle into his arms.

Muley appeared overcome with gratitude. "I really appreciate this. Hope the wife gets better."

"She'll be fine."

Lester clambered down into the boat and took his place behind the wheel. Then Muley untied the bowline and waved good-bye to Ryder. Turning around, he stepped across toward the boat, missed it by two feet, and disappeared. Ryder ran to the railing, looked downward, and saw nothing but Muley's cap floating on the bayou. Then the little man surfaced, blubbering and spitting and grasping for the boat's gunwale.

"He don't handle whiskey too good," Lester apologized for his friend. "He need to stick wid beer." Pulling his friend over into the boat like a sack of wet feed, Muley waved to Ryder, started the engine, and headed down the bayou.

"That coulda been real trouble," Ryder muttered, watching the boat wallowing along as Lester roared with laughter. Glancing back to his right, Ryder saw the bateau carrying Caleb, Laura, and Billie round the curve into sight. *No! No! No! Not now! If they see those girls they'll know we're the ones. . . . No matter how drunk they are, they'll know.*

Ryder stepped quickly through the doorway, returned with the AK–47, and lay prone on the wooden deck in the shadow of the houseboat. He threw one quick look at the bateau behind him, then shouldered the rifle, bringing the front sight carefully to bear in the center of Lester's shoulders just above the back of the seat. *Don't turn around. Don't turn around.*

At that moment, Lester shoved the throttle lever forward. The boat leaped with a roar out of the trough it had been plowing and skimmed along the surface of the bayou. Soon it had all but vanished from sight in the slight chop and the sunlit glitter of the waves.

———

"I'm not sure about this job, Jack. How much money can there be in a little grocery store in Napoleonville?" Caleb sat at the table on the houseboat's deck. Above him the white moon was a thin, curved scar on the black sky.

In the glare of a butane lantern, Ryder studied a map spread out on the table. "I studied this place real good. They cash payroll checks every Friday." He traced a route on the map with the tip of a thick forefinger. "I saw enough money crossing that counter last week to keep us going for a long time."

"You know the cops are watching everything closer now. Won't they have a deputy or somebody around on a day when there's so much money in the store?"

Ryder folded the map and shoved it aside. "There wasn't nobody there last Friday." Tapping the map with his finger, he said, "You did a good job getting that map. It's got every little bayou and canal in the Basin on it."

"Thanks," Caleb said, then returned to the subject of armed robbery. "I don't know, Jack. Maybe we ought to lie low for a while." He glanced toward the cabin where Billie and Laura were sleeping. "Let things cool down a little."

"Maybe you ought to get a job selling shoes."

"What's that supposed to mean?"

Ryder jabbed a thumb at the cabin behind him. "Ever since you brought that rich brat out here, you been finding something wrong with any job I plan. There ain't no sure thing in this line of work. A man could—"

" 'Line of work'?" Caleb interrupted him. "You make it sound like we're plumbers or carpenters or something. This ain't work. It's nothing but taking money from people who *do* work."

Ryder's knotty hands, lying on the table in front of him, curled into fists. "If you're turning into a yellowbelly on me, maybe you oughta strike out on your own."

Ignoring his brother's insult, Caleb thought he finally saw a possible way out. "There's something I've been meaning to talk to you about, Jack. Now's as good a time as any." He glanced at his brother's rigid arms, his dark eyes glinting like chunks of polished coal in the lantern light. "Why don't we let Laura go back to live with her mama?"

"You really are losing it, boy."

"What's wrong with that?"

"Wanda ain't never gonna lay eyes on that little girl if I have anything to say about it." Ryder's voice spilled over with fury. "She ain't fit to be a mama or a wife. She proved that when she run out on both of us."

"You didn't leave her much choice, Jack."

"You better watch your mouth, boy!"

"It's the truth. After that last time you beat her up, she was afraid you were going to kill her." Caleb watched his brother's blazing eyes. "She told me so herself."

Suddenly Ryder clutched the table with both hands, stood up, and sent it clattering across the deck. The lantern thudded against the wood, rolled against the railing, and went out.

Turning over backward in his chair to avoid the flying table, Caleb lay on the deck staring up at his brother. He watched the fingers of his strong hands curl outward and thought for a moment he was planning to throttle him.

"Laura Lee ain't going nowhere! You can stay or you can

pack up and leave. Which is it?"

Caleb knew that it would be only a matter of time until something terrible happened to Laura if she remained alone with her father. "I'll stay."

PART THREE

—

LEAD ME HOME

11

Rebel and Tiger

Dylan gazed at Erin sleeping peacefully in the incubator, then suddenly his eyes refocused, seemingly of their own accord, and he saw between himself and his daughter a faint reflection of a man in his late twenties, shaggy haired and hollow eyed, in the glass wall of the incubator. *That's about what I feel like*, he thought, *not a real flesh-and-blood person, just a thin, insubstantial image trapped inside a wall of glass.*

"Sweetheart, do you feel all right?" Susan sat almost knee to knee in a chair directly in front of him.

"I'm fine," Dylan replied automatically. He turned from his daughter to his wife. Anyone could see that sleepless nights and concern for her only child had taken its toll on her. But Dylan saw something more in his wife's pale face, framed by its tangle of dark hair, something more fragile, more vulnerable . . . and more lovely than ever.

"How's the case going?"

Dylan gave her a weak, weary smile. "The National Guard made a sweep through the Basin yesterday."

"That's good, isn't it?" Susan said naïvely. "I mean, the more people you have trying to find these men the better it is for everybody. Isn't that right?"

"Not always."

"I don't understand."

"If that bunch didn't run these guys off it's a miracle. Fighting a war and investigating murder and armed robbery cases don't have very much in common." Dylan felt the weight of the past few days pulling on him like gravity.

"But surely they must have done *some* good," Susan insisted, her eyes trained on the slow, regular breathing of her child. "With all the training they've had, they should be able to handle two men, even if these men are cruel and heartless enough to gun down a priest and a harmless storekeeper."

Dylan gazed at a miniature Christmas tree standing on a table in the anteroom. The tiny star in its crown somehow lifted his spirits. "Its just a different ball game, Susan. The bad guys don't wear different uniforms or speak a different language or sound a bugle before they attack."

"I just wish the whole thing was over with. You can't keep spending all your days on the job and all your nights here at the hospital."

Dylan found himself caught up in his brief treatise on law enforcement and the courts. "And when you finally do track them down and get the cuffs on them, you can't just shoot them or stick them in a prison camp. You've got to grind and polish and sand them into the right shape so they'll fit into the correct slot in the legal system."

A monitor began its insistent bleeping at the far end of the aisle of incubators. A nurse with short gray hair and the trim figure of a schoolgirl whooshed by on crepe-soled shoes.

Dylan turned back to Susan and finished his soliloquy. " 'Cause if you don't, the system just spits them right back out on the street, and you start all over again."

Susan had slipped her hand through the porthole and was gently brushing Erin's fine tendrils of blond hair back from her ears, tiny replicas of her own.

Guess she lost interest, Dylan thought. *Can't say that I blame her. I was beginning to bore myself.*

"I didn't mean to ignore you," Susan said, smiling at her

husband, "it just seems that I can't go more than a few minutes without touching her."

"Don't worry about it," Dylan said, his eyes dazed by sudden loss and long hours. The dozens of people he had questioned about the robberies all seemed to run together in a blur of faces and a drone of voices; their words as senseless as the two murders. And always he carried the image of his infant daughter lying behind the glass walls that held life inside her tiny breast. "I find myself carrying on these mindless blabberings before I even realize it." He suddenly grasped Susan's hand.

"What's wrong?" She slipped her hand from the porthole and placed it on his cheek.

"I just had a horrible thought!"

"What is it?"

"Maybe I'm being transmogrified"—he looked at her with mock alarm—"into an insurance agent . . . or maybe one of those screaming car salesmen on the television commercials."

Susan slipped her hand away from his cheek and gave his earlobe a sharp tug.

"Oww. . . !" Dylan flinched at the quick pain. "The nuns at Holy Name used to do that."

"Well, don't scare me like that again! I thought you were having a heart attack."

"I couldn't have a heart attack. I'm still just a boy," Dylan said, although at this burnt-out end of his long day, he had started to feel like an old man.

Susan smiled and nodded at the youthful, gray-haired nurse as she returned from the monitor at the end of the aisle. "Everything all right?"

"Nothing serious," the nurse said. Then she took a better look at the young couple watching over their child. "Can I get you folks something? Coffee, hot tea. . . ?"

Susan shook her head and turned back to Erin, engulfing the tiny hand in her own.

"I'd sure appreciate a cup of coffee," Dylan replied, "with a little sugar if it's not too much trouble."

"Be right back."

Dylan watched Susan caressing their daughter, murmuring words of love and comfort, then softly humming a lullaby. *I wonder if Erin hears her. I hope so.* Suddenly he seemed to see the incubator as a glass coffin, child sized and ready to be lowered into the dark, bottomless chasm of a grave. He fought against the terrible image in his mind . . . and against the desire to rescue his daughter from the incubator.

Susan said in a voice soft and wistful, "I look at Erin and I see her in so many ways: her first birthday party with all the family and friends gathered around, and her grinning at the big cake with its one tiny candle; her little face lighting up on Christmas morning when she sees all the presents around the tree; splashing in a wading pool in the yard with white clover blossoms and yellow sunshine everywhere." She turned to Dylan, her green eyes shadowed with the fear she struggled to keep out of her voice. "I even see her coming down the stairs in her prom dress, and she's so lovely it hurts me to think about it."

"Here's your coffee."

Dylan smiled at the nurse and took the cup of rich, dark coffee. "Thanks. You're a lifesaver."

The nurse smiled at Dylan's unintended pun. "That's what all the babies tell me"—she glanced about at her small charges—"or they would if they could talk."

"How do you think Erin is doing? Any chance we can take her home soon?" Dylan watched the answer forming in the depths of the nurse's clear gray eyes. Then they seemed to cloud over with a secret knowledge that she would not form into words.

Unable to hold Dylan's gaze, the nurse looked down at his child. "She may have to stay with us for a little while longer. The final decision is always left up to the doctor"—she forced a smile—"and the parents, of course." With an affectionate pat

160

on Susan's shoulder, she made an efficient about-face and walked away in a rustle of nylon.

Dylan stared at Susan's profile, thinking how much it reminded him of a cameo his grandmother used to wear. Her skin had that same warm glow of old ivory that had somehow been transformed into soft, warm flesh. As he stared at her he saw a single tear form in the corner of her eye, then spill over and trace a glistening path down her cheek.

Wearing boots, Levi's, and a brown leather jacket, Dylan entered the little cafe to the sound of the bell tinkling above the glass door. The jukebox was playing another song that had been popular before Dylan's birth. "Don't you have any songs on that thing less than thirty years old?" he asked to the sound of Judy Garland's pure, sweet voice, vaguely remembering the scene in the old black-and-white movie with her singing to a picture of Clark Gable.

"You made me love you, I didn't want to do it. . . ."

"There ain't been a song in the past thirty years *worth* puttin' on my jukebox." Jesse clattered a plate down on the counter in front of a young man with shoulder-length brown hair and a glazed look in his eyes.

"Thanks." With a furtive glance at Dylan, the man hunched over his hamburger and hash browns protectively and ate as though he were being timed for speed.

Pulling out a chair at a table in the front, Dylan sat down and stared out the plate glass window. Two minutes later, Ike walked in and spoke to Jesse, then, taking his gray sport coat off, hung it on the back of a chair, and sat down across from Dylan. As though this were a signal only he had knowledge of, the young man gobbled the last of his hash browns, dropped two crumpled bills on the counter, and scurried out the door.

Ike watched him leave. "You think I did something to offend him?"

"I think he smelled your badge."

"There's a distinct possibility that boy may be experimenting with controlled dangerous substances," Ike said as the man passed the window with a final glance behind him.

"You want some coffee?"

"Yeah." Ike turned to wave at Jesse who was cleaning the mess off the counter and mumbling about the man's eating like a pig and smelling worse than one.

"I'll get it," Dylan offered, standing up. "Jesse's got enough to do cleaning out the sty." Walking around behind the counter, he poured two cups of coffee, stuffed a dollar into Jesse's shirt pocket, and returned to the table.

Stirring sugar into his coffee, Ike said, "You know, you could probably make more money as a waiter than you do in the law enforcement business."

"Not me," Dylan replied, "not with all these late-night holdups. It's too dangerous."

"It ain't so bad," Jesse said from behind the counter, his hands submerged in soapy water. "I ain't been shot but once." He spoke over his shoulder. "You get some strange types coming in about three in the morning, though."

"What do you mean, strange?" Ike asked, taking a sip of coffee, then making a face at his cup.

"Well," Jesse continued, splashing soapy water out onto the floor, "take the cat that came in here about three weeks ago. It was 3:06. I remember 'cause I knew as soon as I saw that crazy look in his drugged-up eyes that I was gonna need the time for the police report." He began drying dishes and stacking them beneath the counter.

Dylan looked at Ike who merely shrugged, then said, "Well, aren't you gonna tell us what happened?"

"Oh yeah," Jesse said, wiping his hands dry on a dish towel. "I almost forgot. This cat walked up to the counter, pulled a sawed-off shotgun from beneath this long coat he was wearing, and said, 'Two family orders of fried chicken . . . to go, please.'" He sat on a stool and leaned his elbows on the counter. "And that's what I mean by strange people coming in around three in the morning."

"That's a real interesting story, Jesse," Ike said, winking at Dylan.

Jesse didn't miss Ike's skeptical wink. "If it ain't true, there ain't a catfish in that Mississippi River behind me."

"If you say so," Ike nodded, digging inside his coat pocket and coming out with a thick manila envelope. He opened it, slipped a stack of papers out, and laid them on the table. "I've got some things here you might be interested in. Things like size nine and a half and red."

"What in the world are you talking about?"

"I said I'd give you his shoe size and favorite color, didn't I? Well, you just got 'em."

Dylan leaned forward, sorting briefly through the police reports, photostats, and official Department of Defense forms. "Looks like you've got a pretty sizable file on our boy. How'd you track him down?"

"A lot of it was just pure luck," Ike admitted. "We got a break on the camper they were using. A New Orleans cop making a routine check for stolen vehicles found it in a used car lot. As it turns out the truck wasn't stolen. It actually belonged to Jack Ryder—that's his name, by the way—but the license plate was from a truck stolen in Townsend, Tennessee."

Listening in on the conversation, Jesse added, "Ain't we got enough crooks down here in Louisiana without bringin' some more in from Tennessee?"

Ike frowned at the intrusion, then returned to his stack of papers. "After we got the truck, the rest was just the computer whizzes whacking away at their keyboards."

Dylan slipped a black-and-white print from the middle of the stack. A man in his early twenties, wearing a campaign cap and a wide grin, posed in front of an American flag. The eyes didn't quite pick up the smile that posed on the rest of the face. "So this is the one-man crime wave. Looks like your typical all-American boy, doesn't he? Or he did back then."

"I think he's seriously disturbed, Dylan."

"What makes you say that? Robbery and murder aren't always committed by psychopaths." Dylan stared at the picture. "Maybe he's just hard-down mean."

Picking up a DOD form, Ike scanned it and tossed it back in the pile. "He was in the First Cav in Vietnam. Saw some real tough combat against the NVA."

"So did a lot of other men."

"I think combat did things to him, though, that it didn't do to most men," Ike said, staring out the window at the empty parking spaces along the street.

"Like what?"

Ike kept his gaze on the deserted street and sidewalks. "There's reason to believe," he glanced at the papers, "if their information is correct, that he wasn't satisfied with merely killing the enemy soldiers. He did some pretty weird things to the bodies after the battle was over."

An image flashed through Dylan's mind: an unlit cigarette dangling from a twisted mouth, granny glasses framing unseeing eyes, and a New York Yankees baseball cap set at a cocky angle on the head of an NVA soldier slumped against the side of a hooch deep in the jungles of Southeast Asia. "Things like that weren't all that uncommon, Ike."

"You must be kidding," Ike said, his eyes fastening on Dylan's. "I can't understand something like that."

Dylan saw no good purpose in continuing that part of their conversation. "Can I get this picture out to the other sheriff and police departments?"

"Yeah," Ike nodded. "I cleared it with our office this afternoon. There's a picture and some information on the brother in here that we got from his high school." He slipped the papers back into their envelope. "The FBI's always glad to lend a hand to local law enforcement."

"Especially when the locals work the case and you don't have to chase around after these guys."

"Especially then." Ike grinned and slowly pushed the envelope across the table to Dylan.

———

Dylan pulled the little Volkswagen into the shed next to the bayou, turned off the windshield wipers, and killed the engine. The downpour on the tin roof made Dylan feel as though they were inside a boxcar roaring through a dark tunnel. "Well, here we are. You glad to be home?"

Susan stared out the open doorway leading onto the dock. Rain beat down on the weathered boards and churned the surface of the water to a frothy whiteness.

"Susan . . ."

"Oh, sorry." She shivered slightly and held her wool coat against her chest with both hands. "Yes, I guess so," she hastened to add, "but I want to go back to the hospital first thing in the morning. There may have been a change during the night."

"Maybe you should stay home for at least one day before you go back, Susan." Dylan took one of her hands. It was cool and moist. "You need to catch up on your sleep a little. The nurse said they'd call if there's any change."

Susan slipped her other hand over Dylan's. "I know. It's just that Erin's so . . . so little and all alone in that big hospital." She turned her eyes toward Dylan. Sorrow seemed to have sifted like a fine, dark dust into their green depths. "I know she can tell when I'm not there with her."

"Okay," Dylan relented. "Maybe we should wait until this rain lets up a little before we go to the house."

"Fine with me," Susan agreed, pulling the collar of her coat up around her neck and settling back into her seat. "We can make believe we're on a date at the drive-in." She pointed through the windshield. Pewter-colored light spilled in the doorway from outside. "That can be the theater screen turned on end and we'll watch *December Day on the Bayou*. That always was one of my favorite movies."

"It's not bad," Dylan said, feeling the chill leaving Susan's hands as they absorbed the warmth of his own body. "And the stereo sound effects are great."

"Remember when we were first married and I'd make us some sandwiches and iced tea to take with us to the drive-in movie? That was fun, wasn't it?"

Dylan nodded. "I don't think you ever made it through an entire show without going to sleep."

Susan let her breath out in a whisper of a sigh. "It seems like such a long time ago."

"Yeah. They won't be around much longer."

"You really think so?"

"Yep. People are getting too used to air conditioning," Dylan said, staring through the windshield at the make-believe screen for their imaginary movie. "Most of us can't handle the summer heat anymore, even at night. And the winters are too cold and rainy. So . . . they're on the way out."

"Sometimes I think that things were better before we had so many creature comforts."

"Good. I'll disconnect the air conditioner. It'll save a pile of money on utilities next summer."

"Of course, I could be wrong about *some* creature comforts," Susan admitted in a level voice.

"We'll lose the Rebel drive-in first," Dylan continued, glad to see a touch of Susan's sense of humor returning. "They're going to build a big interchange on the Airline where it is now; part of the I–110 spur heading north out of town."

"The Tiger won't be around much longer, then," Susan added. "There was hardly anybody still going there when we moved down here." She reached over and took Dylan's hand, squeezing it gently. "I'll miss them."

Dylan left the subject of drive-ins on that nostalgic note. "I'm going to see Mr. Verrett first thing in the morning. We'll go to the hospital as soon as I get back."

"I hope Billie's all right . . . and the little girl they have with them." Susan brushed her tousled hair back from her face. "You think he can find those men?"

"If anybody can. I'm going to take him some copies of their pictures that Ike got for me. He needs to know some more things I found out too."

"Then we can go to the hospital?"

Dylan nodded. "Don't worry. I'm leaving at daylight so we'll have plenty of time."

Leaning her head on Dylan's shoulder, Susan placed her arm around his neck. "She's so precious . . . and so tiny. . . ." Her soft words were almost lost in the sound of rain and the December wind moaning around the eves of the shed.

Dylan felt his wife's body shaking softly against him. Turning toward her, he encircled her with his arms. Sobs rose from her breast as hot tears wet his cheek pressed against hers. Just as he had felt the warmth of his own body flowing into her, warming her hands, he could now feel her grief; her terrible sorrow flowing into him, becoming his own.

"This fella looks like he could have some devilment in him all right." Alton Verrett placed the picture of Jack Ryder on the table and picked up the one of Jack's younger brother. "This one, though . . . he's got a wounded look about him. I imagine he's taken some pretty hard knocks in his short life."

Dylan sat across the table in a ladder-backed chair. He gazed out the window at the frost-burned weeds, the trees still dripping with rainwater, and the winter sun's pale glow against the early morning sky. "I'd treat both of them alike if I were you, Mr. Verrett."

"This one's not a bad sort," Verrett said, gazing at Caleb Ryder's picture. "He's a sensitive boy if his eyes tell me anything at all. Reminds me a little of Alan Seeger."

"The name sounds vaguely familiar?"

Verrett gave Dylan a look of disapproval. "You should know him, young St. John. He was a poet and American aviator during World War I." He placed the picture on the table and gazed back through the years. "Made his reputation primarily on the basis of one poem, 'I Have a Rendezvous with Death.'"

"I *have* heard of that. Think I may have even read it a time or two years back."

"There may be hope for you yet."

Dylan tried to pull Verrett out of the poetic past into the grim present. "You think you can give us some help with these guys, Mr. Verrett?"

"I'll find 'em."

"You're that sure?"

"Yep, I'm *that* sure." Verrett turned his faded eyes on Dylan. "I've got one condition."

"Sure."

"When I do find these boys, it's just you and me going after them until the girls are safe."

"I don't know if Emile will go along with that or not."

Verrett shoved the pictures back to Dylan's side of the table. "Tell him to find 'em himself, then."

"You really mean this, don't you?"

"You don't know much about me if you think otherwise." Verret's eyes held a flinty light. "You let the word out where these men are and there'll be more firepower heading into these swamps than we had at the Battle of Beleau Wood. There'd be no way to keep those girls from getting hurt."

Dylan knew Verrett meant every word. Remembering Judge LeBlanc's National Guard fiasco, he found himself beginning to agree with the old swamper. "Okay. We'll do it your way. But we've got to have backup as soon as the girls are safe."

"That's your problem." Verrett reached over and picked up the pictures. "Let's have a quick cup of coffee. Then I'm going to check out a few likely spots." He gave Dylan a boyish grin.

"The kind of places where Butch Cassidy might hide out with his Hole-in-the-Wall Gang if he'd been pulling his train robberies down here in South Louisiana."

"You'll let me know as soon as you find them. . . ."

"That's what this is all about unless you lost me somewhere," Verrett said, getting up and walking over to his wood-burning stove. He poured two cups of coffee and set them on the table.

"How are you going to get in touch with me?"

Verrett sat down and sipped his coffee. "Soon as I find 'em, I'll go over to Jack Miller's Landing and telephone you. The sheriff's office will know where you are, I suppose."

"Yeah. I'll have the department's boat on standby. I think it's fast enough to catch anything they're likely to be in."

"Fine. It's all settled, then." Verrett smiled and his face looked almost like that of a boy's suddenly taken by wrinkles and white hair. "Now . . . I found a poem in that new book you gave me I think we oughta discuss a bit. It's called 'Aspects of Robinson' by a fellow named Weldon Kees."

"I've read him."

Walking across the room, Verrett picked up the book from a table next to his bunk, then sat back down across from Dylan. "This man doesn't think much of the modern world."

Dylan sipped his coffee, staring at Verrett over the top of his cup. "That's probably why you like his work."

Verrett nodded slowly, then said, "He talks about all the money and gadgets and fancy clothes, but they only cover"—he opened the book and ran his forefinger down a page, stopping when he found the right line—" 'His sad and usual heart, dry as a winter leaf.' What a great line! That's about how I felt when I was living in town. I'd be surprised if this fella hasn't left it all and found a place in the wilderness somewhere."

"He left all right."

"What do you mean?"

Dylan lowered his cup to the table, staring into it. "Back

in 1955 his car was found abandoned on the approach to the Golden Gate Bridge. He's never been heard from since."

Verrett started to speak, then slowly closed the book and gazed out the window at the bone white sky. "No wonder I like his work so much."

12

THE GETAWAY

Dylan watched Susan slip out of her white surgical gown and leave the little anteroom. He glanced through the glass at Erin. She stretched her legs and rubbed the side of her face with a tiny fist. Then she lay still and serene as though she had just been put down for a nap; as though blood no longer seeped into her brain from a ruptured vessel beneath fine white-blond hair and the thin, frail bone structure.

"How's the new father tonight?"

"Just fine," Dylan said, looking up at the nurse. Her short gray hair held a healthy sheen beneath the neon glow, and her smile was warm and genuine.

"She's a good baby," the nurse said, glancing at Erin. "When she gets out of this place, you'll find she was more than worth all the long nights."

Dylan nodded. "By the way, I never got your first name," he said, glancing at the word Chenevert in black letters on her white plastic name tag.

"Actually, my first name is two names. All my friends call me Rose Marie."

"How about Rosie? I kind of like that."

"So do I." She smiled again, then her gray eyes softened as they held Dylan's. "I just want you to know I've been praying for Erin. Of course, I pray for all of our little ones, but somehow she's been kind of special to me."

"I sure appreciate that."

"See if you can talk your wife into getting a little more rest. It won't help things if she ends up back in the hospital."

"I'll try, but it was hard enough persuading her to go down and get a bite to eat."

"I'll speak with her," Rosie said and walked away toward the bright anteroom and on toward the nurse's station.

Slipping his hand through the porthole, Dylan gently stroked Erin's silky hair with his fingertips. She made a face at him in her sleep. He smiled, touched her pink cheek, then took his hand away and picked up Susan's Bible that she had left on her chair. Slipping his finger beneath the bookmark, he opened it to the page she had been reading in the book of Second Samuel.

Dylan began to read the story about King David committing adultery with Bathsheba and then having her husband slain in battle, and he found himself getting lost in its message when Bathsheba bore David a son. He knew what David felt like when the child became sick, and how David pleaded with God for the life of his child, then he "fasted, and went in, and lay all night upon the earth." When the child died, Dylan saw, to his surprise, that David ceased to weep and fast. Instead, the first thing he did after washing and anointing himself was that he "came into the house of the Lord, and worshipped."

"I can't imagine anyone having so strong a faith that he could worship God immediately after the death of his son," Dylan whispered to himself, then glanced at Erin and shook his head. David's agonizing words rang in his own heart: *"Can I bring him back again? I shall go to him, but he shall not return to me."*

Neon brightness glinted off the glass walls of the incubator. From a certain slant, it appeared to Dylan that the tiny form inside was radiant with light. He imagined himself watching Erin on the playground at some sun-drenched park as he had other children: riding the miniature merry-go-round; climbing the ladder and slipping down the sliding board, her little girl's voice spilling over with musical laughter and squeals of pleasure.

Then suddenly reality engulfed him like a cold vapor and he knew . . . he may never see his daughter play with other children; may never even hear her laughter or see her eyes light with joy at the sight of a frisky, bouncing puppy or a new doll in a frilly dress. He stared at the tiny form beneath glass. *This may be all your mother and I ever have of you, Erin. You may never know how much we love you. . . . And even this may not last much longer.*

"Father, I don't understand why . . . why Erin has to be so sick. How could Susan ever bear it if. . . ?" Dylan's voice was hushed, barely a whisper. "It seems like I've been fighting one thing or another all my life." He brushed at the corners of his eyes. "But this is something that I'm not strong enough to handle. I'm just too tired . . . and too weak. I always thought I was strong . . . but now I know I'm not. I'm not strong at all."

Dylan bowed his head. All around him was the rush of air through oxygen bottles; the steady hum of a generator somewhere beyond the walls; and on the next aisle the weak cry of a child. But his mind registered none of these sounds.

"Lord, you were looking out for me all those years when I wasn't even thinking about you. I see that now. There's no other way to explain how I got through the war . . . and all those other messes I got myself into.

"Jesus, right now I turn my life over to you. I'm sorry I've made such a mess of it, and I ask you to forgive me for all the things I've done wrong. If you let Erin live, I'll be the best daddy I can be for her, and you already know that she couldn't have a better mother than Susan. No matter what happens, though, my life is yours from now on, Jesus." He raised his head slowly, gazing at his daughter in her cradle of light. "And if Erin . . . if Erin dies, then just like David said about his son . . .

one day we'll go to be with her."

————————

The wind howled in the eaves of the cabin, sending snowflakes swirling past the windows. Inside, Laura sat on the linoleum floor staring at the colored lights bubbling away on the Christmas tree. She could hear her grandmother moving about in the kitchen. The rattle of pans, the whisper of the flour sifter, and the smell of baking made her feel warm and safe as though her grandmother's love had become a part of the sounds and the sweet fragrance of the Christmas cookies.

A deep rumbling sound drew Laura away from the safe haven of dreams. She opened her eyes slowly, raising up on one elbow. In the bunk beneath her, she heard Billie throw back the covers and swing her feet onto the floor. Then she saw her put her clothes on and quietly leave their cramped little bedroom at the back of the houseboat.

Slipping into one of Caleb's old flannel shirts that she used as a robe, Laura clambered down from the bunk, stood in the shadowed doorway of the hall, and watched Billie pouring coffee at the two-burner stove.

Billie took a sip of coffee, then saw Laura. "Morning, sugar. You want some breakfast?"

"No, ma'am. Not right now." Following Billie over to the door leading onto the houseboat deck, she peered out through the screen at her father and uncle.

"This is some boat!" Ryder stood with his hands on his hips, his partially buttoned fatigue shirt splayed open over his round belly. He stared down at the sleek black-and-silver fiberglass runabout powered by an eighty-horse Mercury. "We'll be able to leave the local swamp boys like they was tied to a post."

Caleb sat behind the wheel, grinning as though his brother's words were gem stones tossed to him with no strings attached. "It's a beauty, ain't it?"

"How can you afford such an expensive boat?" Billie

stepped through the cabin door holding a cup of steaming coffee. She had on sun-faded bell-bottomed jeans and one of Caleb's khaki shirts. "That thing must have cost you a year's salary."

"Same as anybody else." Caleb saw an image of himself only a few hours before, hot-wiring the boat's starter in the shadows of a high dock while above him drunken laughter and jukebox music spilled out the door of the honky-tonk into the night. "Bought it on time. It's the American way."

Billie gave him a skeptical look, but she turned to Ryder when she spoke. "Y'all must make pretty good money out on the rigs just to have credit for a boat like that."

"We do all right," Ryder muttered, his eyes roving over the boat, "if it's any business of yours."

"It is pretty," Billie admitted, turning back toward Caleb. "Why don't you take me for a ride in it?"

"This boat's for business," Ryder grunted, reaching inside his shirt and scratching his chest. "You ain't gonna make it just another one of your little play toys."

Billie glared at Ryder, her face flushing with banked anger. Then she let it out. "I'm getting tired of you ordering me around, Jack. You aren't my boss, and you certainly aren't my daddy."

Ryder took a step toward her, his own anger blazing in bloodshot eyes. "You'll do what I tell you to, you little brat, or you jist might end up"—he jerked his thumb backward toward the trackless sloughs and backwaters—"with the snappin' turtles havin' you for supper!"

Billie's sudden flush of anger gave way to an expression of fear, her face going pale and her hand seeking the delicate hollow of her throat as though protecting it from Ryder's icy stare. She gave Caleb a pleading look. "Are you going to just sit there and let him threaten me like this?"

Caleb stepped carefully out onto the deck of the houseboat, his eyes darting from Billie to Jack and then back to Billie. "Just settle down, sweetheart. Jack doesn't mean anything by it. He just gets upset sometimes." He turned toward his brother, trying to sound casual. "Isn't that right, big brother?"

Billie carried her coffee over to the table behind Ryder, sat down, and gazed out at the thin morning mist that hovered over the smooth surface of the bayou.

"I'll tell *you* what's right, *little brother*!" Ryder kept his eyes on Billie as he spoke. "If you can't control your *sweetheart*"—twisting his mouth, he made the word sound like an insult—"she's gonna drop plumb off the face of this ol' world one day."

"That's it!" Billie stood up, scraping her chair back on the rough flooring. "I'm going inside to pack and then you can take me home, Caleb. That's the last threat I'm taking from this illiterate sadist!" Then she took one step toward the door.

Ryder spun around on the balls of his feet, the back of his hard hand striking Billie across the cheek. She staggered backward, hit the side of the cabin, and fell to the wooden deck, her eyes glazed with shock. Then sudden, bright tears brimmed over and flowed down her cheeks. She noticed the shadowy image of Laura behind the screen, then gave Caleb the look of a wounded animal, helpless before its tormentor.

Hurrying over to her, Caleb knelt on one knee and helped her to her feet. With his fingertips, he gently touched the red welt Ryder's blow had left on the side of her face. His hands curled into fists at his sides. Suddenly he turned and swung a long, looping right at his brother's face.

But anger had caused him to strike out blindly, and Ryder easily sidestepped, grasped Caleb's arm, twisting it behind his back, and forced him to his knees. With a cry of pain, he glanced over at Billie. She looked at him with pity in her tear-bright eyes, then slowly stood up and disappeared into the cabin. The screen door banged shut behind her.

Laura backed away and let Billie pass. Then she watched her hurry down the short hall into their bedroom, slamming the door shut behind her. Stepping back to the door in the houseboat's shadowy interior, she felt almost as though the happenings in the sunlit world on the other side of the screen were merely part of a television show or a scene from an old movie.

Ryder turned his brother loose, then glared down at him. "See what you made me do? If you can't handle your woman, then I reckon somebody's got to do it for you."

"I'll take her home like she asked me to." Caleb stood up and took a step toward the cabin door. "She doesn't deserve to be treated like that."

"Hold on, little brother!"

Caleb stopped, took a deep breath, and turned around, his eyes grown remote, filling with an icy light. "She's right. You don't have any right to tell her what to do."

"I've got every right. And I'll tell you why . . . just once." Ryder's voice sounded brittle, as though it might break apart in his throat. "That girl knows right where we are. One word from her and every cop in six parishes will be on us like white on rice."

"Next time you touch her I'll stop you," Caleb said flatly, "one way or the other."

Ryder grinned at Caleb as though he had just said something very funny. "Tell you what. You keep her in line and I'll lay off her." He sat down at the table and drank from Billie's cup. "Soon as we decide to move on"—he turned his crooked smile on Caleb—"then we'll turn her loose. Nothing she can do to hurt us then. She won't have no idea where we're going next."

"Just keep your hands off her . . . that's all."

But Ryder had more important things on his mind. "Time for us to go back on the oil rigs."

Caleb gave him a puzzled look, then remembered the deception that had been his own creation to keep Billie from finding out the truth of what they were doing. "Yeah," he said, a disconsolate tone in his voice. "Back to the rigs."

Ryder downed the last of the coffee. "There's this little restaurant down in Thibodaux. On Saturday night they don't close till two in the morning, and they do a business you just wouldn't believe. Now, the way I got it planned . . ."

Dylan threw the gearshift into reverse, backing the sleek speedboat through a partial screen of overhanging, moss-laden branches into a small bayou that opened off the main waterway. The V–8, inboard-outboard engine rumbled and growled with power. "I don't think they'll see the boat back in here if they happen to pass this way."

Fishing a chunk of Fleer's Double Bubble gum from the bib of his overalls, Verrett nodded his head to the right and said, "They're about a hundred yards down the bayou. Good cover all the way." He chewed contentedly. "But we're going to have to be patient. This could take a while."

Dylan eased the .45 automatic from beneath his Marine field jacket, checked the clip, slid it back into the handle, and shucked a round into the chamber. Shoving the heavy pistol back into his belt, he said, "We may have to be satisfied just getting Billie away from them. Getting both of them at the same time's going to be a tricky business."

"That just might be enough," Verrett said, gazing across the bayou at the pink sky above the tree line. "A man's not going to bargain with his own daughter, not even a murderer."

"So if it comes to it we'll settle for Billie. They'll have to run for it when they find out we're here." Dylan looped the bowline over an overhanging limb. "Then we just keep them in sight and use the radio to give our location to Emile and the men in reserve."

Verrett nodded. "They'll have to go ashore somewhere eventually. Then we've got 'em."

"It's possible that both men would leave together," Dylan wished out loud. "That sure would simplify things."

"It's possible they'd see the error of their ways and become Trappist monks," Verrett said with a grin, "but I don't hold out much hope for that."

Dylan grinned back in spite of himself. "You ready to get this over with?" he asked, glancing at the brightening sky.

"Yep," Verrett replied, chewing contentedly.

Dylan picked up the M–16 that lay next to him on the seat, took a full clip from the cargo pocket of his field jacket, and shoved it home. Sliding a round into the chamber, he stood up. "You sure you don't want to bring a weapon?"

Verrett glanced at the twelve-gauge riot gun clipped beneath the boat's dashboard, then shook his head. "I shot at enough men in France to last a lifetime. Besides, you got enough firepower there for both of us."

Dylan felt the same prickling at the back of his neck and the same cold hollowness in the pit of his stomach that had always gripped him just before he went into combat. Holding on to a limb, he stepped out of the boat, then crept carefully along the bank in the direction of the houseboat. Sodden leaves and decaying limbs made little sound beneath his boots. Walking in a crouched position, he pushed aside the branches and undergrowth, stopping every three or four steps to listen.

When Dylan sighted the houseboat through the maze of tree trunks, vines, and underbrush, he glanced behind him at Verrett, pointed ahead with his forefinger, and jerked his thumb downward. Then he got down on his belly and inched forward, pulling himself along with his elbows, the rifle cradled in his bent arms.

Fifteen minutes later, Dylan peered around the base of a massive cypress. The back of the houseboat was only ten feet from where he lay, tied off with yellow nylon rope between two cypress knees. A small wooden table sat on the narrow rear deck between two aluminum folding chairs webbed with blue-and-white nylon bands. He motioned to Verrett, who crawled

just past him, concealing himself behind a thick stand of pal-
mettos.

"Now we wait," Dylan whispered.

Verrett nodded casually, lying flat on the spongy ground,
then rested his chin on his folded hands.

Dylan heard the distant whine of an outboard. A green bateau, cluttered with fishing equipment and carrying two men
wearing baseball caps, skimmed over the dark water out in the
center of the channel. An alligator gar, its yellow-white belly
gleaming in the early light, rolled over next to a clump of lily
pads about twenty feet from shore.

The houseboat rocked in the swells of the passing boat followed by the sounds of someone moving about inside. A marine toilet flushed. Pans clattered faintly in the kitchen. Ten
minutes later a door on the far side of the houseboat opened.
Someone yawned loudly, then coughed. A chair scraped across
the wooden deck.

An hour later Dylan saw Billie LeBlanc, wearing jeans and
an oversized khaki shirt, her face thick with sleep, carry a cup
of coffee carefully down the narrow walkway alongside the
houseboat and sit down in one of the aluminum chairs on the
rear deck. She pushed her tousled hair away from her face with
the backs of her fingers, then sipped the coffee, her puffy eyes
gazing blankly into the shadowy forest.

Dylan slipped his shield out of his jacket, flipped open
the holder, stood up slowly, and held it out toward Billie. Her
eyes widened, her mouth flew open as though someone had
shoved a needle into her spine. Then she stood slowly up,
took two steps over to the rail, and leaned as close to him as
she could.

"Aren't you Mr. Emile's deputy?" she whispered.

Dylan nodded and glanced toward the front of the houseboat. "Where's the girl?"

Billie pointed toward the door leading into the small back
bedroom.

"We're here," Dylan nodded at Verrett who had stood up

slowly from concealment, "to take you home. You think you can get the little girl to go with you?"

Billie shrugged, then gave a furtive glance over her shoulder. "I'll try."

"We've got to get out of here in a hurry," Dylan whispered urgently, his eyes covering the narrow walkway leading to the rear of the houseboat.

Billie eased over to the rear door and grasped the handle, twisting it back and forth. Then she looked helplessly back toward Dylan.

"See if you can get her to open it." Dylan mouthed the words, fearing someone up front would hear.

Turning around, Billie tapped lightly on the window next to the bunk beds. She waited a few seconds, then tapped again, this time slightly louder. The curtains parted and Laura's pale face appeared behind the smeared and cloudy glass. Lying on the top bunk, propped on her elbows, she smiled at Billie, then looked puzzled as she saw the two men standing in the shadows at the edge of the woods.

Billie held her hand palm outward toward Laura, stepped over to the corner of the houseboat, and took a quick look toward the front. Then she hurried back to the window and motioned for Laura to climb down and open the back door.

The sound of the front door opening startled Billie. She froze, her hand on the back door handle.

"Hey! What's goin' on back there?"

Dylan saw Ryder stick his frowzy head around the corner of the houseboat. "I said what's—"

"Let's go!" Dylan yelled to Billie.

Ryder appeared to be in a mild state of shock, a look of disbelief on his face. Then he jerked backward, disappearing behind the wall. "Caleb! The cops are in the woods. Grab a gun and let 'em have it!"

Billie clambered over the rail, stepped onto a huge cypress root rising out of the water, ran across it, and leaped to the bank. Dylan grasped her with one hand, ushering her toward

Verrett who now stood directly behind him.

"Get her to the boat!" Dylan shouted.

"Come with me, child! You're safe now." Verrett grabbed Billie's hand, running with her back along the shoreline he and Dylan had traveled earlier.

Dylan watched them go, then turned around just as Ryder stepped around the corner of the houseboat, his feet spread in a crouched position, holding his AK–47 waist high. Yelling like a madman, he fired a full twenty-shot clip at Dylan. Pieces of bark, leaves, broken limbs, and chunks of mud whirled and scattered through the air as rounds from Ryder's weapon hummed past like mad hornets.

Flattened against the backside of the big cypress, Dylan shouldered his M–16 and stepped out into the open as soon as the clatter of the AK–47 stopped. He found Ryder's chest in the sight of his weapon, his finger tightening on the trigger. At the last moment, he raised the barrel, sending a short burst above the man's head, tearing apart the corner of the building. Ryder dove for cover as blocks of wood and chunks of shingles exploded against the railing and the deck and sailed out into the water.

Dylan saw the fleeting image of a boy of eighteen standing in the open back door, the barrel of his automatic pistol pointed harmlessly toward the floor. Then he whirled around and followed Verrett and Billie along the wooded bank.

At the boat, Dylan said to Billie, "We're going after them. You'll be safe if you stay right here. I'll get someone on the radio to pick you up."

"I'm afraid! I want to go with you," Billie wailed, her face bloodless in the deep shade.

Dylan heard the stutter of an outboard engine turning over, the sudden growl as it caught and started. He glanced at Verrett. "Stay with her!"

Verrett was already untying the bowline as Dylan leaped into the boat and turned the ignition key. The big V–8 caught immediately, rumbling with power. Dylan shoved the throttle forward. The boat leaped almost out of the water, leaving a roiling cloud of mud in its wake.

Breaking through the overhanging brush and limbs, Dylan felt the cool wind in his face, the surge of power that sent the sleek fiberglass hull skimming and bouncing across the smooth surface of the bayou. In the distance he saw the black-and-silver speedboat glinting in the sunlight, its wake rolling out past its sides like foaming white wings.

Dylan kept one hand on the wheel as he grabbed the mike of the shortwave with the other. He gave a brief account of what had happened, his position, and the location of Verrett and Judge LeBlanc's daughter.

Emile's voice came over the radio. "Good work, Dylan. We're closing in on your position right now."

"I'll keep you posted for any change of direction. There's a hundred bayous and pipeline canals he could turn into around this area."

Dylan could now see the men clearly. Their expressions told him they knew he was gaining on them. The man who had fired at him sat behind the wheel. He yelled at the younger one, his face a mask of rage. The child sat on the backseat, covering her head with her arms.

The driver grabbed his rifle off the seat beside him, pointing it one-handed toward the pursuing boat. Dylan eased back on the throttle and cut the wheel sharply to the left, watching the bullets spatter harmlessly into the water in front of him. Then he accelerated again, keeping a safe distance between him and the other boat. He spoke into the mike, advising his backup of his situation.

Dylan watched the driver throw his weapon onto the floorboard, stand up, and force the young man to take the wheel. Then he went to the back of the boat, suddenly lifted the child in both arms and flung her far out into the water. She hit the surface, skittering and tumbling, then disappeared beneath the surface.

Dylan felt a sense of unimaginable horror, cold and relentless in his chest. With one quick look at the diminishing speedboat, he kept his eye on the exact spot where the child had vanished. Cutting the engine, he threw the anchor overboard, jerked his boots off, and plunged into the dark water.

13

CINDERELLA

Susan pulled the Volkswagen into a parking space in the hospital lot, turned the engine off, and gazed out at Capitol Lake, glittering in the pale yellow December sunlight. After a few minutes, she got out, walked wearily up to the front entrance and into the lobby, waving at the receptionist.

Young and blond and bubbling with energy, she said, "You're five minutes late today. I'm afraid we're going to have to dock your paycheck."

Susan smiled, feeling ancient in the face of such youthful enthusiasm. She rode the elevator up to Neonatal ICU, got off, and headed down the hallway.

Suddenly Rose Marie Chenevert spotted her and came charging down the hall, her reading glasses swinging from the silver chain around her neck.

Oh, Lord! What could be wrong? Susan felt a sudden, cold sinking in her chest. Then she saw the beaming face of the nurse and hurried to meet her.

"Oh, I'm so glad you're here!" Rosie clasped both of Susan's hands, then placed an arm around her waist and ushered her quickly down the hall.

"What's happened?"

"Only the best thing you could think of," Rosie trilled. "Erin's awake and grinning like a little possum."

Sudden tears flowed down Susan's cheeks. She felt her heart leap within her and, without remembering how it had happened, found herself in the anteroom, pulling her surgical gown on, rushing toward the incubator. Staring down through the glass, she saw Erin, her gray-blue eyes open, unfocused as yet, but open and staring at her small world. Then her head turned toward Susan, and her mouth opened in a toothless smile.

Susan felt suddenly dizzy as she sat down and slipped her arm through the porthole, stroking her daughter's tiny face. But most of all, she felt a soaring sense of joy almost as though her body was suddenly filled with warmth and comfort and light, and an ineffable, sweet, unending peace. Time lost meaning as she sat gazing at her daughter, at her every move, lost in the wonder and the miracle of life.

"She's going to be a handful. I can see that already." Rosie handed Susan a cup of hot tea.

Forcing her eyes away from her child, Susan slipped her arm from the porthole and took the cup. "She can be whatever she wants as long as she stays healthy."

"She got the stamp of approval from the doctor earlier this morning." Rosie sat down across from Susan. "I tried to call you, but you'd already left."

"How did it happen so quickly?"

"It happens this way . . . or not at all. The doctor said that the bleeding could stop of itself, and that's exactly what happened." Rosie seemed almost as grateful and excited as Susan. "And as far as he can tell, there are no complications at all."

"Well, praise the Lord!" Susan sighed, letting her body completely relax for what seemed like the first time in ages. She sipped her tea contentedly.

"Where's your husband?"

"He had to leave before daylight this morning. They're supposed to have a good lead on the men who've been robbing businesses in the Basin."

"I've been reading about that pair in the newspaper," Rosie

said. "Aren't they the same ones who kidnapped that judge's daughter?"

"She's supposed to be with them." Susan's thoughts focused on telling Dylan her marvelous news. She could almost see his face. "Whether she was kidnapped or not hasn't been determined yet as far as I know."

"Won't your husband be happy! I can already tell he's going to be a good daddy."

Susan nodded. "I wish I could get in touch with him right now, but he said I wouldn't be able to until he finished whatever it was he went off into the Basin to do."

Rosie stood up. "Well, I guess I'd better get back to work." She gazed down at Erin, now sleeping peacefully. "It's times like this that make me remember why I went into nursing in the first place."

"Can I ask you one question before you go?"

"Certainly."

Susan gazed expectantly into Rosie's face. "Do you think we'll be able to take her home for Christmas?"

"I don't see why not."

"Truly? You really think we can?"

Rosie placed her hand on Susan's shoulder. "It's always up to the doctor, but from the way he was talking this morning I think he'd be willing to go along with it."

Susan nodded, cradling her cup in both hands. She sipped her tea and gazed at her child.

Rosie smiled and turned to leave.

"Rosie . . ."

"Yes . . ." She gave Susan a puzzled look.

"Thanks for being such a good friend."

She nodded, started to speak, then smiled and headed in the direction of a complaining baby on another aisle.

———

"You did good work out there today, Dylan." Emile, his charcoal gray tie loosened against his white shirt, sat behind his desk in the slatted light streaming in through the blinds on his office window. "I didn't know if you could pull it off or not."

Dylan slouched in an oak chair next to the wall. "I let them get away, Emile."

Shaking his head, Emile spoke in a level voice. "You know how many times we come out ahead in a hostage situation?"

Dylan, knowing the question didn't expect an answer, gazed blankly through the blinds at the crepe myrtle tree next to the window and rubbed his chin.

"Not many," Emile continued, "and you can check the FBI statistics on that. How's the little girl?"

Dylan met his boss's gaze. "The doctor over at the clinic said she's undernourished, but other than that he gave her a clean bill of health. Even her teeth are okay."

"Well, Elaine's gonna make a good start at taking care of the undernourished part. When they get back here she'll be packed full of gumbo and fried catfish."

Dylan repeated the question he had asked when he came into the office. "No word on those boys, huh? None of the other departments made any contact."

"Not yet, anyway." Emile shuffled through a stack of papers. "Don't worry, we'll nail them."

"They're heading west."

Emile looked up from his papers, then shoved them aside. "How do you know that?"

Dylan took a crumpled road map from inside his jacket, stood up, and smoothed it out on the desk. "See these pencil marks? They're not very plain and they don't follow any particular road. It just looks like they were made by somebody trying to plan a route west and tapping the pencil on the paper as they talked it over."

"Did you show this to anybody else?"

"Yeah. It's already on the air." Dylan refolded the map and sat down. "But I don't think the roadblocks and the BOLOs are going to do much good."

"Why not?"

"This guy who's running the show knows what he's doing. He's gonna take nothing but back roads, travel at night, then find a place to hole up until things quiet down."

"How do you know? He just might go barreling down the interstate, try to put as much distance between him and the Basin as he can."

"Just a hunch," Dylan admitted. "But I think I know something about how his mind works. He's like a hunted animal now and he's going to head for the desert places. Keep away from people as much as he can."

"There's going to be a lot of cops out there looking for these guys," Emile said hopefully.

"Yeah," Dylan replied, a resigned tone in his voice. "Guess I'd better check in with Susan," he said, reaching for the telephone. "Told her I'd call soon as I got in."

The phone rang before Dylan could pick up the receiver. Emile answered it, then handed it to Dylan. "It's Susan. You two must be on the same wavelength."

Dylan listened to his wife's voice. Her words seemed to come from another dimension where miracles still happened; one completely unfamiliar to him. Then the good news finally broke through the wall that had guarded his heart. "She's really going to be all right? The doctor's certain? I'm on my way." A smile lighted his tired face as he hung up. "Erin's okay."

Emile shot out of his chair and clasped Dylan's hand, clapping him on the back. "That's great news."

Dylan suddenly felt stunned, almost numb. Already the conversation with Susan seemed like a dream. "Yeah, it *is* great news, isn't it?"

"You going up there like that?"

Dylan looked down at Emile's wrinkled uniform he had exchanged for his soaked clothes. "Why not? There's nobody in Baton Rouge I'm trying to impress."

"Here she is, folks." Elaine walked into the office holding Laura's hand. "Evangeline's answer to Cinderella."

Dylan smiled down at the beaming child. Her scrubbed

cheeks carried a pink glow, and her hair was squeaky clean and shiny. She wore a new blue dress that matched her eyes. "My goodness, you must be a movie star."

Laura blushed and giggled, then held out her arms for Dylan to pick her up.

"Looks like you've made a real friend here, Dylan," Elaine said, smoothing the child's dress.

"We got to be good buddies on the boat ride out of those swamps, didn't we, Laura Lee?" Dylan cradled the little girl in his arms, brushing her gleaming hair with his fingertips.

She nodded, gazing with a childlike wonder into Dylan's eyes. "Yes, sir."

"Tell you what, Laura Lee Ryder," Dylan said. "How'd you like to go see a pretty little baby with me?"

Laura grinned, nodding her head rapidly up and down.

Elaine's expression clouded slightly. "The Child Welfare people are looking for a temporary place for her."

"We're not going to worry about that," Dylan assured her. "I've still got a few contacts with those folks. Susan and I might just keep Laura Lee with us for a few days." He looked at the child in his arms. "How'd you like that?"

Again her smile answered for her.

"Our first Christmas in Evangeline." Susan sat next to Dylan on the sofa watching Laura ride her three-wheeler around the living room, weaving through the bright and crumpled wrapping paper, scattered toys, ribbons, and opened boxes. Then she spun away down the hall toward her bedroom, the ribbed plastic wheels thrumming on the hardwood floor.

"Our first Christmas as parents," Dylan said, slipping his arm around his wife.

Susan smiled at the sleeping child in her arms, then looked at her husband. "I think I'm enjoying the dolls as much as Laura did," she said, her face aglow. "I get to be a mother and a child at the same time. This is so much fun!"

Dylan felt a sense of deep peace flowing over him as though the troubles of the past had been little more than a dream within a dream, lost now in the miracle of Christmas and the joy of birth. The change in his life was not lost on his wife.

"Something's happened to you, Dylan."

He turned to his wife with a grave expression that crumbled beneath the weight of the miracle, replaced with the smile of a ten-year-old boy. "What do you mean?"

"You know exactly what I'm talking about. You've been smiling now for days like some invisible person is always whispering something funny in your ear."

"Beats me." Dylan shrugged.

"It started even before we found out that Erin was going to be all right."

Dylan called back that night at his daughter's side when he had laid his life . . . and all of its troubles . . . down at the foot of the Cross. "You already know what happened to me."

Susan's eyes sparkled with tears. She slipped her hand inside her husband's. "Yes." Her voice was as soft as the slow December rain whispering in the trees outside the window.

"I wanted it to be a special Christmas present for you."

"It is. It truly is."

Dylan had no words for the love that he felt for his wife at that moment, or for the peace and joy that had come into his life as a gift that night in the hospital. He gazed at his sleeping child, then brushed the tears from Susan's cheeks with the back of his finger and gave her a kiss.

From the kitchen radio came the sound of a children's choir singing about the birth of another child long ago: "Yet in thy dark streets shineth, the everlasting light . . ."

Dylan looked at the tree, its lights and sparkling ornaments watched over by the bright angel in its crown; listened to the slow rain on the roof; smelled the rich, sweet fragrance of the Christmas pies and cookies on the kitchen table; felt the warm, reassuring presence of his wife and child next to him, and realized that for the first time in his life he was truly content.

Susan finally broke their silence. "Do you think there's any chance we could adopt Laura, Dylan?"

Dylan picked up his mug of hot chocolate from the floor and took a sip as he listened to the tinkling sound of Laura's toy xylophone drifting down the hall. "The Child Welfare people are going to try to get in touch with her mother through their interstate compact right after the holidays. We'll just have to wait and see what happens."

"Do you really want to?" Susan stroked Erin's cheek with her fingertips. "After all, we're still new to this parent business, and having two at once . . ."

"I think it's kind of a fun business to learn about," Dylan said. "Don't you?"

"Two at once, though?"

"But they're so *little*." Dylan grinned. "I think we can handle two *this* small."

Susan's soft laughter spilled over as she said, "I'm not quite sure I follow your logic on raising children, but you sure do make it sound like a lot of fun."

"It'll be even better than that."

"We shouldn't tell Laura anything, though"—Susan glanced toward the hallway—"until we know something for sure. Maybe they'll find her mother or . . ." She let her words trail off.

"You never can tell in cases like these. I had a little experience indirectly with foster care and adoption cases when I was in juvenile work." Dylan took another swallow of chocolate, then placed the mug back on the floor. "The only thing you knew for certain was that you never knew anything for certain."

"Sounds like you don't hold out much hope."

Dylan shrugged, then shook his head slightly. "I'm only saying that things could go either way. It might turn out to be very simple or very complicated . . . or impossible. There're just too many variables with cases like this."

"But we could give her such a good home," Susan insisted,

glancing at her child. "Just like we're going to do for Erin. Doesn't that mean anything?"

Dylan nodded his agreement. "Sure it does, but it doesn't guarantee anything. I've seen children taken out of great foster homes and placed back with parents who continue to abuse them just like they always did." His voice held a slight edge of frustration as he continued. "You never know how the judge's going to rule when it comes to court; then there's the case-workers, some do a good job and some of them ought to be taking orders at Burger King. Next you have to run the whole gamut of supervisors and managers and even departmental heads in some cases."

"It all sounds so complicated."

"That's an understatement," Dylan admitted. "And in Laura's case there's the interstate problem. That just doubles the number of people and the amount of red tape." He took a deep breath. "And that's not even considering the problems we could run into with Laura's family."

Susan waved her hand as though blowing all the bureau-cratic smoke away. "Let's not talk about that anymore." Then her face softened. "You know what Laura told me last night when I was putting her to bed?"

"Hmmm . . . let me guess. That you had the best-looking husband in South Louisiana."

Susan made a tolerant face at her husband's crack, then said, "That she wishes you were her daddy."

"She said that?"

"I think when you pulled her out of that bayou it was al-most like giving her new life." Susan stared out the window at the gray December morning. "She was so close to dying and then the next thing she knew she woke up in your arms."

"She really has fit right in with our family. Almost like she's been with us all of her life."

"I think Laura's background has made her a very dura-ble"—Susan seemed to be seeking the correct word—"and a very *tolerant* child."

"The ones that make it through situations like she's had to cope with usually turn out one way or the other," Dylan went on, "very fragile or, like Laura, very durable."

Susan smiled warmly. "And she's got so much love stored up inside her that sometimes it just bubbles over."

———————

Susan gazed at the poster of a serene angel keeping watch over two children walking a rickety bridge across a dark chasm. Santa Claus had given the print to Laura for her birthday. She now lay sleeping peacefully beneath it in her new bed. Leaning over, Susan kissed her on the forehead and headed down the hall to the other bedroom. She heard the sound of the rocking chair and Dylan's voice singing "Amazing Grace" as a lullaby for his daughter.

As Susan entered the room, Dylan stood up with his daughter and lay her in the baby bed that his parents had bought just before his birth. The walnut finish was shellacked, its gleaming surface decorated with pictures of teddy bears.

Dylan covered Erin with a pink blanket, kissed her goodnight, and followed Susan down the hall. In the kitchen he said, "What a great Christmas!"

"The best ever," Susan agreed. "I haven't had so much fun since I was a little girl."

"Sure saves me a lot of trouble." Dylan sat down at the table, folding his arms on the yellow Formica top.

"Trouble? What do you mean?"

"Now I don't have to try and figure out what to get you for your birthday," Dylan said, combing his dark hair back from his face with his fingers. "A tea set, a toy stove and sink, and a Betsy-Wetsy doll."

"You think that's funny?" Susan grabbed a dish towel from the rack on the wall, twirling it tightly between her hands.

Dylan shoved his chair back and sprinted from the kitchen, but she popped him sharply on the behind as he rounded the corner into the living room.

"Ow! That thing oughta be considered a deadly weapon. You're better with it than Linus is with his blanket." He came back in, rubbing his wound, and sat down.

"Anybody for pecan pie?"

"You have to ask?"

But Susan had already cut two slices from the pie tin on the counter. Placing them on saucers, she set them on the table and poured two foamy, cold glasses of milk. "We've got another whole pie to finish after this," she said, sitting down.

"What a shame," Dylan said, forking a chunk of the rich brown crunchy pie into his mouth. "The things I do for my marriage," he mumbled as he chewed.

"Don't talk with your mouth full."

Dylan swallowed and took a drink of milk. Picking at the crust with his fork, he gave Susan a solemn look. "I need to find the man who killed Nick, Susan."

She stopped her fork halfway to her mouth. "But . . . I thought he left the state."

"He did. That's the problem." Dylan dropped his fork on the saucer. "Nobody's gonna go looking for this guy, Susan. The cops in the other states will see the sheet on him when it comes in on the teletype . . . and forget it in about two hours. Then if he gets stopped for a traffic violation, they'll run a license check; maybe get him that way unless he's changed vehicles or plates, which he probably has. He's gonna be real careful now."

"But," Susan grasped for a way to keep Dylan home, "you don't have any authority outside of Maurapas Parish . . . do you?"

"Not now, but I will before I leave."

"I don't understand. You're Emile's chief deputy, but that's only for this parish."

"The governor can have me cross-designated as a law enforcement officer in another state. All he has to do is make a phone call to the governor of the other state." Dylan made a steeple of his hands, resting his chin on his fingertips. "In this case it would be for both New Mexico and Arizona."

"Sounds too simple."

"I thought so, too, but Emile said it actually works. He used it four or five years ago."

Susan took another tact. "You keep saying 'he.' I thought there were two men involved."

"Only one killed Nick."

"How do you know?"

"I saw them both, Susan. I know who killed him." Dylan went back to the bedroom, returning with the crumpled map, which he spread out on the table. "See right here?" He pointed with a pencil to a spot on the map.

Susan came around and sat on his lap, gazing down at the map. "Deming, New Mexico. So what?"

"Lean a little closer. You see those marks? They're real faint, so look close."

Susan leaned closer, squinting slightly. "Yeah, I do see them. They look like somebody made them by tapping a pencil point in the area around Deming."

"Exactly." Dylan leaned back in his chair, one arm around Susan's waist. "Somebody who had decided where they were going and emphasized it by tapping the area with a pencil."

"That could be pure speculation on your part."

"You sound like a schoolteacher now."

"I am a schoolteacher, and I don't think a few marks on a map is proof of where this guy is."

"It's all I've got, Susan," Dylan admitted reluctantly, "except for one thing."

"What's that?"

"I was in the service with a guy from Lordsburg"—he tapped the map with his finger—"a little farther west here. He talked about the country down south of there. Said it was as barren and desolate as the backside of the moon."

"The kind of place you think this guy would pick to hide out in."

Dylan nodded. "I've got a gut feeling about it, Susan. I just know that's where he's gone." He moved his finger east and west in the area below Lordsburg and Deming, and just across the Arizona border. "Somewhere in here." Looking into the depths of Susan's green eyes, he said, "I won't go if you say not to."

Susan traced the side of his face with her fingers. "I couldn't do that. You have to do this for Nick." She put her arms around his neck and kissed him softly on the mouth, then lay her head on his shoulder, in the circle of his arms.

14

DESERT PLACES

Dylan hummed along New Mexico Highway 9 in his blue Volkswagen between endless stretches of sand, scrub brush, and rocks. Ahead of him a spume of dirt and sand whirled out of the brush and across the highway. When he had stopped for gas in Las Cruces, the attendant had told him the Southwestern Indians saw evil spirits in the whirlwinds and sang aloud if one crossed their path. "That's why they're called 'dust devils' today in New Mexico and Arizona," he'd said.

Watching the miniature tornado vanish as suddenly as it had appeared, Dylan remembered the words of the man in the grease-stained overalls who had pumped his gas. Dylan had seen no evil spirits in the wind, and he certainly felt no urge for singing in this desolate, end-of-the-world country.

Off to the south, Dylan glanced at the Big Hatchet Mountains, dark and foreboding in the night's final hour. Ahead of him he saw the tiny town of Hachita sitting in the shadow of the mountains, its tin roofs reflecting the day's first red glow. Glancing at his map, he saw that the town sat just south of the Continental Divide where it bends east and west.

Hachita, facing an abandoned railroad bed and locomotive water tower, proved to be a community cluster of clay bricks, wood, aluminum, and rusting scrap metal. Abandoned automobiles sat baking in sandy lots between dilapidated house trailers and adobe shacks.

Dylan passed a small grocery store with a black-and-tan hound asleep on its porch, then pulled into the rutted parking lot of the only other business in town, the Badlands Bar and Filling Station. Gazing at the buttressed adobe saloon, he almost expected to see John Wayne swagger out the door, six-gun hung low on his hips, tilt his hat back at a rakish angle, and say, "Morning, Pilgrim. What brings you to these parts?"

Inside, Dylan encountered no gunfighters in the long room with its round, leather-topped poker table and L-shaped bar. One man in a threadbare denim jacket and boots that looked as though they had stepped out of the nineteenth century sat at the bar swilling beer like soda pop.

"Morning," Dylan said, sitting three stools down from him at the bar.

The man, whose face the desert sun had taken a particular dislike for, turned and said, "What's so dadburn good about it?" then returned to business.

"Don't pay him no mind." A blade of a man with a missing eyetooth that didn't seem to bother his warm smile stood up from behind the bar. "Stoke down there," he nodded toward the drinker, "couldn't find a good word to say about Santa Claus on Christmas morning; could you, Stoke?"

Stoke turned his head slowly, gave the bartender a crooked smile, and took a long swig from his tall glass.

"Name's Ray Waters. What'll it be?" He held out his callused brown hand.

"Dylan St. John." He shook hands and said, "I could sure use a cup of coffee."

"What . . . no cracks about Waters in the desert?"

Dylan smiled thinly. He felt drugged from hours of staring at white lines on unending ribbons of black highways. "I imagine you've heard enough without mine."

"Ain't that the gospel." Waters poured coffee from a glass carafe into a chipped brown mug. "Makes you kinda special in my book. Here, hope it's not too strong for you. It's been simmering since four o'clock."

Dylan gazed at the calendars, old license plates, and beer signs hanging on the mirror behind the bar. He sipped the coffee. "Tastes kinda weak to me."

"Weak? You from Turkey? I hear they make the strongest coffee in the world."

"South Louisiana."

"Second strongest," Waters corrected himself. "I was down in that Cajun country one time working out on the oil rigs. Went to a place called Lafitte. Woman in a cafe brought me a cup of coffee that dissolved the spoon when I stirred some sugar in."

"I've been there," Dylan said, rubbing his eyes with thumb and forefinger. "I couldn't drink it either." He swallowed more coffee, staring bleary eyed at the antlers and paint-by-numbers western scenes on the wall to his left.

Waters proved to be tenacious in conversation. "Looks like you ain't slept in a while. You got business in these parts?"

These parts. Dylan thought of John Wayne again. "Drove all night," he answered. "I'm glad you asked. My mind's so fuzzy I almost forgot why I stopped."

"And I thought it was 'cause you'd heard about my world-famous coffee."

Fishing Jack Ryder's picture out of the pocket of his field jacket, Dylan placed it on the bar. "I'm a deputy trying to track down this man. Thought he might have passed through here."

Waters ignored the picture. "We ain't had no local law around these parts since Pancho Villa used to raid the county from down in Mexico. You a real deputy?"

Dylan took his badge out of his jacket, opened it, and held it toward Waters.

"Well, I'll be . . ." He picked up the picture and made a face at it. "He was in here all right." Handing the picture back, he said, "That feller give me the creeps."

"When was he here?"

Waters scratched the back of his head with a gnarled fore-finger. "About five . . . maybe six days ago. Bought a whole case of whiskey. Paid for it from a roll of bills that would have choked a half-grown mule."

Dylan leaned forward on the bar. "You remember anything he had to say? Anything that might have indicated where he was headed?"

"He didn't have much to say, as I recall. Kinda surly, if you know what I mean." He glanced down the bar. "Sorta like ol' Stoke over there, but not just grumpy either." He gave Dylan a knowing look. "This 'en was stomp-down mean."

"Did he do anything out of the way?"

"Not exactly," Waters admitted. "It was just . . . just the way he handled hisself, I reckon. Like he'd just as soon put a bullet in your gut as he would shake your hand." He glanced suspiciously around the nearly deserted room as though Ryder might be hiding in it somewhere. "I've seen his kind before, and they all carried guns . . . jist like he did."

Dylan raised his eyebrows a quarter inch, creating twin fur-rows between them.

"That's right." Waters answered Dylan's unasked question. "I seen that hogleg sticking in his belt beneath his shirt. Looked like a .357 to me. A mean gun."

"Anything else you can tell me?"

"There was a boy with him . . . stayed out in the car, though."

"About eighteen? In a green Ford?"

"Right on both counts."

Dylan felt a cold prickling at the back of his neck. "Did you hear him mention anything about where he might be going . . . a town, a highway number, anything at all?"

Rubbing the gray-and-brown stubble on his bony chin, Waters muttered, "Hmmm . . . I think he said they come down through Alamogordo right near the valley where the gover-mint blowed off the atomic bomb back in July of '45." A shadow crossed his face as he looked at Dylan. "You ain't superstitious, are you?"

"No. Never was."

"That's good, then. The place he come by where that bomb went off," Waters lowered his voice as though he were in a confessional, "the Spaniards call it the 'Journey of Death.' I just thought you ought to know, you being on a journey after that fellow with the mean eyes."

"Thanks," Dylan said flatly. "I appreciate your concern. Anything else you can tell me?"

"Said he was going to Paradise."

"What's that?"

"Town just over the border in the Chiricahua Mountains past Portal. Used to be just a hole in the road. I expect there ain't nothing much left to it now. He probably seen it on his map."

"Any place for them to put up in that direction?"

"Not this side of the mountains. When he put the whiskey in the trunk of his car I seen some camping equipment. Lots of places to camp around there."

Dylan swallowed the last of his coffee. "You've been a big help, Mr. Waters."

"I think that's kinda funny, don't you?"

"What's funny?"

"That feller taking the Journey of Death through the Portal to Paradise."

"You're a regular Bob Hope, Mr. Waters." Dylan slid off his stool and headed for his car.

Waters chuckled and called out as Dylan stepped through the door, "You come back to see us again, young feller. I can tell ol' Stoke there really took a liking to you."

———

Continuing west on Highway 9, Dylan marveled at the arid, empty loneliness of the desert; stoic mountains and crumpling hills, scrub brush and rocks. A flat tire brought him closer to the land. It seemed to tell him that he'd better keep on moving if he wanted to survive; that all it had to offer him was blinding sun, biting cold, and bitter desolation.

Driving through Playas he saw a scattering of house trailers; a little farther on he came to Animas where the Indian children were making a ruckus on the playground of a rundown school. Then the road turned, and he headed directly across the flat desert toward the towering rock spires of the Chiricahuas.

Crossing into Arizona, Dylan saw alongside the numberless road a rough wooden sign with an arrow pointing west to Portal and Paradise. There appeared to be nothing ahead but solid stone walls and towers and outcroppings rising from the desert floor. Dylan saw no way through it, then the road made an abrupt right-angle turn, and a wide cleft opened up in the mountains.

Driving on through the canyon, Dylan saw that it was barely wide enough for the road and a small stream, its banks lined with juniper, pine, sycamore, and white oak. Above him through the trees, he could see the canyon walls of yellow and brown and orange rock rising vertically for hundreds of feet. The cooling shade and the sound of the water rippling across the stream bed made a strange impression on him. He had the feeling that he had traveled hundreds of miles away from the desert rather than having made a simple right-hand turn.

Farther on, the town of Portal held several rock buildings and not one single human being. Three miles later, Dylan drove the little Volkswagen across the stony bottom of Cave Creek and pulled into a grove of sycamores on the opposite bank. He built a fire, cooked an early supper of bacon and eggs and bread grilled in the skillet, then spread his sleeping bag on the ground next to the creek and sipped his coffee from a tin cup.

Listening to the water gurgling past in the stream and smelling the pungent scent of the evergreens as he rested in the black shade, Dylan wondered at so marvelous a creation. This cool, peaceful oasis lay nestled in the northeast corner of the trackless Sonoran Desert.

"You sure picked a pretty place to camp."

Dylan struggled hand-over-hand from the depths of sleep toward the circular glow of light that was his waking. Propping up on one elbow, he saw a man wearing an improbable outfit of fringed leather leggings, a soft doeskin shirt, and a headband with a single turkey feather dangling from a thong at the back. "Evening. I didn't know anyone else was around."

"Been here a week," the man said, jerking his thumb backward past the side of his head, "parked on the other side of the road next to those big rocks. You wouldn't notice the pickup unless you walked the creek bank up that way."

Dylan sat up, the sleep draining from his face, and stretched. Afterglow filled the sky above the mountains and drifted down into the glade like a lavender mist.

"Reggie Whitman," the man said, a toothy grin on his bland face. He sat down on a slab of rock next to the sleeping bag. "From Silver City. That's over in New Mexico."

Shaking hands, Dylan introduced himself. "That's a different kind of outfit you've got there."

"A passion of mine," Whitman admitted proudly, adjusting his feather. "I teach high school history. The American Indian and the Old West desperadoes are my favorites. I come out here in the ancestral home of the Chiricahua Apache and"—he looked slightly embarrassed—"just kind of make-believe that I'm living a hundred years ago."

"Sounds like a good hobby to me. A whole lot better than stamp collecting or building model airplanes."

Whitman grinned, obviously pleased that Dylan approved of his pastime. "You're kind of unusual. When I tell most people, they think I'm"—he tapped the side of his head with his forefinger—"a little touched, you know."

"Probably the same ones whose idea of a good time is leaping out of an airplane at ten thousand feet."

"Never thought of it that way."

Dylan had found it profitable when trying to get information from people to let them relax with casual conversation, but once Whitman got started, it appeared that he could go on all night. He had just taken a breath to continue his treatise on the desert tribes of the Southwest when Dylan turned the conversation around. "You see anyone else come through here in the last few days?"

Whitman looked disappointed that his history lesson had been interrupted, but he smiled bravely and said, "Sure did. The night I got here . . . or maybe the night after."

"Two men; one about thirty and the other eighteen or so, driving a green Ford sedan?"

"Friends of yours?"

Dylan identified himself and gave his reason for wanting to find the men.

Whitman took a deep breath, blowing it out between his lips. "Robbery and murder. Sure fooled me."

Dylan felt that Whitman probably knew a lot more about the past than he did the present. "They seemed okay to you?"

"Well, I only talked to one of them . . . the young one. His name was Caleb, as I recall. He seemed like a real nice young man. Polite, pretty well read for someone with no formal education beyond the tenth grade."

"What about the other one?"

"Yeah, that one," Whitman muttered, shaking his head slowly. "He staggered over to my truck one time to growl something at his brother. The rest of the time he stayed right over there by the creek bank sucking on a bottle of whiskey until he passed out. Next morning they were gone."

"You have any idea where?"

"There's only one road. Goes right over the mountains to Dos Cabezas and Willcox." Whitman pointed down the narrow road that led through the trees and on up into the mountains. "Caleb, the young one, told me they were going up in the high country to camp out for a while."

Dylan gazed down the road leading alongside the creek. "Are there any side roads or trails they could turn off on?"

Whitman laughed. "After a few miles the road isn't anything but a trail. Not a good time of year to be heading up into the high country."

Dylan noticed Whitman's frequent glances toward his coffee pot. "Want a cup?"

"Don't mind if I do." He sat down and held a tin cup while Dylan poured, then leaned back and stretched out his thin legs. "You know, the outlaws of Tombstone used to hide out back here in this canyon. So did ol' Goyathlay."

"Who?"

"It means One Who Yawns."

"Never heard of him."

"I think you probably have." Whitman grinned. "The U.S. Army called him Geronimo. He used to camp out here right by this same stream. That was when . . ."

Dylan knew it was going to be a long night.

Dylan awakened with the mist clinging to the rocks and bushes and drifting out over the water. A dim red glow in the east told him that sunrise was still a half hour away. The night chill had been seeping into him through his sleeping bag and the extra blanket he had thrown on top of it. Making a fire, he washed his face and brushed his teeth in the stream, then sat cross-legged on his folded sleeping bag, sipping his first cup of coffee.

"Morning."

Surprised at the predawn greeting, Dylan spun around, spilling coffee on his hand.

"Sorry. I didn't mean to startle you."

Dylan was startled a second time when he caught sight of Whitman's outfit. He wore a black Stetson, black leather jacket trimmed in silver and turquoise, and a pair of spanking new

Levi's stuffed into tall black cowboy boots. A Colt .45 single-action revolver was slung low on his hips. "You have an amazing wardrobe, Mr. Whitman."

Whitman gave him a sheepish grin. "I thought I'd offer my services in capturing your bandits."

Stunned for a moment by the idea of Whitman joining him in some kind of vigilante rampage, Dylan drank coffee while he thought of a reply. "Well, I'm afraid it's not that simple. You see, you'd have to be deputized by one of the local authorities, and I'm afraid we're kind of short on them out here."

Whitman's face dropped along with his spirits. "But you might need some help. There's two of them."

"I don't think I will. What I plan to do is locate them, then drive into the nearest town and come back with some help. If they're camping out for a while like they told you, I should have plenty of time."

"What if they ambush you?"

Dylan decided it was time to part company with Reggie Whitman. "I appreciate your concern, Mr. Whitman, but I couldn't let you do anything illegal."

"I suppose you're right."

Tossing his gear into the trunk, Dylan turned to bid farewell to the aspiring gunfighter. "It's been nice having your company, Mr. Whitman."

Whitman frowned and scratched his pointy chin. "I think I'd better ride along with you."

"I thought we had this settled."

"Oh, not for that," Whitman protested. "It's just that when the pavement plays out down at the end of the canyon, it's kind of hard to locate the road up the mountain."

Dylan looked into Whitman's eyes, then decided that he had given up his Wyatt Earp role and meant only to be helpful. "Okay. But how do you get back?"

"Walk. It's not far and I always take a morning constitutional anyway."

"Hop in."

Shortly after the pavement played out, Whitman pointed to a barely discernible single lane that bent and twisted up the side of the mountain through the scrub oaks and pines. He sat and stared out the window, then turned toward Dylan. "Thanks for putting up with me."

"My pleasure."

"Most people get their fill of me real quick . . . including the ones I called friends."

Dylan had no idea how to reply, then said simply, "I like you, Mr. Whitman. Don't give up on people. Maybe you just chose the wrong friends."

"Maybe so." He opened the door and stepped out of the car. "Well, adios, compadre."

Dylan laughed, then leaned over and shook his hand through the window. "Adios."

"One more thing. Listen close." Whitman pointed along the faint track leading into the forest. "When you get about halfway up, there'll be a fork in the road. The rock ledge to the left shelved off about two weeks ago, so the highway department made a temporary road to the right around a big pine."

"I'll look out for it."

"No, you don't understand." Whitman leaned in the window and frowned. "You can't see the drop-off till you're right on it. They marked it with a detour sign, but a few days back someone, they don't know who, pointed the sign the wrong way, and a man and his son went over the edge. Be sure to keep on the right."

"I will."

Whitman nodded and stepped back.

Dylan waved as he headed up the rutted, rocky trail. In his rearview mirror he caught one last glimpse of Whitman, a comical, sincere, lonely man standing on the edge of a deserted road wearing an outfit from the last century. Then the trail made an immediate sharp bend to the left, and Dylan glanced out his side window at the road. Whitman had vanished. *There's no way he could have gotten out of sight, even running.* Dylan felt the skin prickling along his spine, but the ruts and craters and rocks soon required all his concentration.

The makeshift road climbed higher and higher, sending the Volkswagen twisting and bending through every point on the compass in ten-minute intervals. Around the sharp turns it looked as though someone had welded the trail to the side of the mountain. Dylan saw nothing but clouds and blue sky out the window. He felt more like a pilot than a driver.

Then Dylan found out why Reggie Whitman had been camping next to him along Cave Creek. Near stupor from fighting the road, he saw a detour sign and wrenched the steering wheel left; then Whitman's face flashed before him and he stomped on the brakes, sweat streaming down his face.

Dylan felt weak, drained, as he pulled the brake and stepped out of the car. Eight steps later he rounded the huge pine and looked a thousand feet down a vertical wall of rock. Far below him, a hawk soared over the tops of the juniper and white oaks on the canyon floor.

15

END OF THE TRAIL

As Dylan drove ever higher into the Chiricahuas, snowbanks lay in the shallow depressions and narrow wadis in the rock and on the shady side of the trees. Soon a few scattered flakes drifted down through the bare limbs of the oaks, and within twenty minutes snow began falling in earnest.

The land gradually began to level off as he neared the summit, but the whole world was quickly turning white. Through the slap of the windshield wipers, Dylan saw a sheltered area in the midst of several huge pines, pulled in, and turned off the wipers. He looked at his gas gauge. Not quite a half tank. After letting the car warm for a few more minutes, he cut the engine. A cracking noise startled him, followed by a heavy thump of a falling limb.

Pouring coffee from a red Thermos, Dylan sipped it slowly, preparing to wait out the storm. Fifteen minutes later, no longer able to see though the frosted windows, he got his sleeping bag and extra blanket out of the trunk. Pulling on a heavy black sweater from his duffel bag on the floor, he curled up in the cramped backseat. He lay there picturing his little lump of a car being dug from beneath a huge snowbank the next day by a highway department snowplow.

The wind howled in the tops of the pines, dropping to a deep moan as the gusts subsided before the next hard blow.

Pulling the blanket over his head, he listened to the wind, felt it buffet and push and jostle the car. At times the storm seemed to wrap its windy arms around the little car and shake it. After another hour he dropped into a warm, enfolding darkness.

The quiet awakened Dylan. A gray light the color of weathered concrete seeped through the snow-covered windows of the car. Feeling stiff and sore from the few hours in his short and narrow bed, he leaned forward, opened the glove box, and looked at the watch he had tossed in there before starting his trip. Noon. It looked more like dusk.

Starting the engine, Dylan poured the last of the coffee, sipping it slowly while he waited for the heater to warm the car enough for him to face another day. As he listened to the whir of the heater, he thought back on the long, hard road miles, the all-night driving, catching an hour or two of sleep in a roadside park, and the people he had talked to along the way. They all seemed to merge into a blur of faces and a babble of voices . . . except for Reggie Whitman. He still saw him clearly in his Wyatt Earp clothes, his sad, vulnerable eyes lighted with kindness.

Dylan killed the engine, pulled on his heavy field jacket and boots, then stepped out of the car into the noonday gloom. The oaks scattered across the summit of the mountain stood bleak and blackened against the relentless white of the high country as though they had been scorched. The remnants of the storm sighed high in the pines.

Walking along the road, visible only by the open trail it followed among the trees and brush, Dylan checked the depth of the snow and decided the Volkswagen could handle it. He would drive slowly along the road, checking every possible exit into the woods, looking for signs of a camp. From what he had seen of the mountain, he felt that there would be no place where they could pull more than fifteen or twenty yards off the road. He gazed at the beauty of the high country, losing himself in its windswept wildness and its vast, imponderable silences.

Dylan had walked almost back to his car when he noticed a sudden movement to his left. Then he saw the green Ford behind a screen of stunted cedars, almost entirely covered with snow, and beyond it a tent, beaten and crumpled by the storm.

"Hold it right there!"

Jack Ryder stepped from behind the gray-black trunk of a pine to the left of the road, the slim, lethal barrel of the AK–47 holding steady on Dylan's chest. "Would you look at this. The boy scout from Louisiana." Ryder's lips curled back in a sneer. "You must want me real bad to track me from them swamps all the way to this mountaintop."

Dylan's hands were stuffed inside his pockets. The heavy automatic inside his belt pressed uselessly against his side. He felt the .45's extra clip, smooth and hard against his hand. Gripping it loosely with his fingers, he tried to fasten his mind around any possibility of escape from the cold stare of the AK–47's single black eye.

Stepping a little closer, Ryder said, "I saw the way you handled that M–16 back there at the houseboat. You coulda plugged me easy, but you didn't. Why is that?"

"Right now I'd have to say it was stupidity." Trying to keep his voice calm, Dylan wondered what Ryder's game was; why he didn't go ahead and finish the inevitable.

Ryder chuckled at the remark, but his eyes remained as cold and fixed as polished chunks of obsidian. "You're probably wondering why I don't go ahead and get it over with. Maybe it's because I saw you jump in that bayou after I chucked my little girl out of the boat; that I'm so grateful I'm gonna turn you loose." He shook his head slowly from side to side. "I ain't."

Dylan had seen in Vietnam what a round from an AK–47 could do to the human body. He could almost feel the jacketed slug ripping through his chest.

"The reason is," Ryder continued with obvious relish,

"that you simply got to die. Any lawman that hounds me for fifteen hundred miles ain't likely to jist turn around and go home . . . now, is he?"

Anything to distract him, Dylan thought, *just long enough to give me some kind of chance.* He glanced again at the gun barrel, unwavering in Ryder's competent hands.

Ryder took several more steps forward. "But it ain't smart to shoot a cop, so I got me another plan. I know you been reportin' in; lettin' people know where you are so when you turn up missin' "—he nodded somberly as though purveying some great truth—"there's gonna be a search and they'll find your body."

Dylan noticed Ryder relaxing as he continued to speak; the gun barrel lowered slightly, wavering to his right.

"And if they find a bullet in you," Ryder continued, "why, then they'll know I killed you, and every cop in this country won't rest till they strap me in the electric chair."

Letting his forefinger extend along the length of the clip, filled with the thick .45 rounds, Dylan grasped it firmly, preparing to throw it with a quick flick of his wrist.

"But if they find you at the bottom of some ravine, they'll think you was jist another dumb flatlander cop that didn't have no business up in these mountains."

"Jack."

Ryder turned to his right as Caleb rose up on the other side of the snow-covered Ford.

Snatching his hand free, Dylan threw the heavy clip with a snap of his wrist, then dove headlong toward a stand of oaks just off the road.

Ryder spun back toward Dylan, the gun barrel tracking his movement. Then he glimpsed a dark blur and felt the shock of the spinning clip tear into the corner of his left eye. Squeezing the trigger of the AK–47, he sprayed a burst in Dylan's direction.

Dylan hit the ground hard, rolling over and over in the powdery new blanket of snow. He heard the clatter of automatic weapon fire, got one quick look at the ground erupting behind him, then scrambled behind the trunks of the oaks. Snatching the .45 from his belt, he elbowed over to the right, leaned just far enough around the base of a tree to see Ryder slogging for cover, and fired three shots at him as fast as he could pull the trigger and adjust his aim, the weapon's recoil jarring his wrist and shoulder. Two of the heavy rounds ripped slabs of bark from the big pine Ryder sprawled behind, while the third went whining off into the woods.

Breathing deeply, Dylan considered his chances. His extra clip lay out in the snow where it had bounced off Ryder's face. He had four rounds left in the Colt. Ryder had a twenty-shot clip in the AK–47 and undoubtedly one or two extras in his pocket. And there was the brother out behind the Ford.

Dylan peered around the base of the tree. A short burst from the 47 hummed past, tearing bark and spanging off slabs of rock. Hoping to catch Ryder off guard, he quickly leaned to his right, the .45 gripped firmly in one hand, found Ryder's dark form at the center of the right angle formed by the dark pine and the white snow with his front sight, and fired once.

Ryder's answering hail of fire was immediate and deadly. One round clipped the receiver of Dylan's .45, flinging it behind him. The shock traveled like an electric current from his hand upward through wrist, elbow, and shoulder. Fragments of the shattered bullet stung his hand and forearm. He scrambled for the pistol with his left hand, grasped it, lay on his back, and saw that the receiver was locked in the open position. Frantically he tried to unjam the weapon, but it was hopelessly locked, the frame bent.

From across the road, Dylan heard the faint snick of Ryder sliding another clip into his rifle. Again he worked at the receiver, knowing it was useless.

Ryder's voice rasped in the cold air. "I think I saw that Colt go flying. Am I right, boy scout?"

Dylan felt a shiver run through him that had no connection with the cold. Staring upward through the filigree of black limbs, he thought of Susan; remembered the night at the hospital, gazing at Erin in her cradle of light. He remembered scenes from his childhood; his father's work-hardened hands gently lifting him; his mother's soft voice in the night. Then he saw only the sky, sealed with high gray clouds.

"Ready or not, here I come."

Glancing around the base of the tree, Dylan saw Ryder coming, doggedly plodding across the fresh snow toward him, holding the rifle at port arms. Lying on his back in the snow, Dylan glanced at the rivulets of blood dripping from his wrist, bright against the powdery snow, and knew it was over.

Ryder stepped cautiously around the tree, the barrel of his rifle centered on Dylan's chest.

Dylan closed his eyes. Suddenly his fear left him. A sense of deep peace flowed through him as though this world could no longer touch him. He heard the roar of the weapon, then he heard nothing at all.

Opening his eyes, Dylan saw a white light. Dazzling. Sunlight through an opening in the clouds, bursting like white fire on the bright snow. Then he heard the sound of weeping. Ryder lay sprawled on his face, a single dark hole in the center of his coat.

Looking to his right, Dylan saw Caleb standing at the edge of the road, staring at his brother's body, the pistol dangling from his hand. He fell to his knees, covering his face with his hands, the pistol clattering against an outcropping of rock.

Dylan drove into the shed next to the cabin on the bayou. Again, as had happened so many times in the past, the sound of rain drumming on the tin roof welcomed him home. After the barren dryness of the deserts of New Mexico and Arizona, he embraced the rain as though it were an old friend.

Getting out of the car, he looked at the duffel bag and the road clutter in the backseat and floorboard, then decided to clear it all out the next morning. He threw the field jacket over his shoulder and walked over to the side door, gazing out at the rain pounding on the white shell path between the shed and the cabin. The kitchen window suddenly glowed with amber light. He heard the door opening out onto the gallery.

"Dylan . . ."

Dylan thought the sound of her voice was like water in a dry and dusty land. "I think so. Maybe you could give me a second opinion."

"Oh, Dylan! You're home!" Susan hurried across the porch and down the steps, then flew toward him along the white path. She carried a black umbrella and wore a long cotton nightgown. Rushing into his embrace, she dropped the umbrella on the shed's dirt floor, threw her arms around him, kissing his lips, his face, and then his lips again.

Dylan stumbled backward into the shed, holding her around the waist, one hand against the wall for balance. "Whew! If I get receptions like this every time, I'm taking all the out-of-state trips that come along."

Susan pressed against him. "I didn't expect you until tomorrow."

"Drove straight through from El Paso," he said, breathing in her warm, summery fragrance. "I missed Erin too much to stay gone another day."

"You missed Erin!" Susan pressed both hands against his chest, staring into his eyes. "What about me?" Then she saw the gleam of a smile lighting his eyes and knew that she had been taken in once again.

Dylan laughed, then glanced down. Susan stood barefoot on top of his boots. "You're gonna get sick."

"I'm going to be just fine, thank you."

He kissed her once more, then spread his field jacket over her shoulders. Bending slightly, he placed his arm beneath her legs, lifting her like a new bride.

Susan placed her hand on the side of his face. "Did you find out what's going to happen to Caleb?"

"I don't know much more now than when I called you from Arizona."

"But he saved your life! That has to count for something, doesn't it?"

"It could mean all the difference," Dylan answered, thinking of Caleb slumped to his knees in the snow, broken with grief that he had killed his own brother. "He has his age going for him, too, and since he was a juvenile back in Tennessee, they've agreed to hold his charges there in abeyance."

"What's going to happen to him?"

"I think the courts here should give him a break because he never pulled the trigger on anybody—except his brother, of course—and because I'll testify on his behalf. But he'll have to serve some time, probably in a minimum security prison."

"I sure hope so. If it wasn't for Caleb, I wouldn't have a husband . . . and Erin wouldn't have a father." Susan shivered slightly, holding the jacket around her with one hand. "Do you think we could go inside now?"

Dylan glanced around the dank, cluttered shed. "I don't know. It's kind of cozy out here."

"Home," Susan said, pointing toward the cabin.

Leaning over so Susan could reach the umbrella, Dylan let her pick it up and hold it over them, then walked along the path and climbed the steps onto the gallery. Setting her down on the plank flooring, he asked, "How're my two little angels getting along?"

"Just beautifully," Susan sighed. "Laura thinks she's Erin's second mother. She's been sleeping with me while you were gone. Said she wanted to be close to her little sister so nothing would happen to her during the night."

Dylan thought of the miracles in his life that had been like love letters from the Father; a wife who had stood by him and loved him when he deserved nothing but contempt; the two children, one a miracle of birth, the other a miracle pulled from the swamp's dark waters; and the two separate times on his journey through the deserts and mountains of the Southwest when his life had been spared.

"You like it out here in the dark?"

The words rose directly from Dylan's heart. "There's never any dark where you are, Susan." He took her in his arms, feeling the warmth and softness of her; feeling the weariness of the road drain away; feeling the empty ache and the lonely, sad desolation of desert places lose all hold on him. He had come home.

EPILOGUE

"Be still, you little wiggle worm." Susan pinched Erin's rosy cheeks, then leaned over and blew imaginary bubbles on her chubby stomach. Erin giggled and squirmed beneath her ceramic mobile of Pooh Bear, Christopher Robin, and the other creatures who lived in the Hundred Acre Wood, then she giggled some more.

Dylan stepped into the room, slipping on the coat to his new powder blue suit that Susan had bought him for Easter. "We need to leave in ten minutes."

Susan gazed down at Erin. "What do you think, chubby? Can you be ready in ten minutes?"

Erin blew bubbles in reply.

"I think that means no," Susan said, turning around toward Dylan. "Oh, don't you look nice in your new suit."

"Nice?" Dylan replied, glancing down at his neatly rolled lapels and sharply creased trousers. "I look like a tall, skinny robin's egg."

Susan laughed, then sprinkled powder from a Johnson's plastic bottle on Erin and rubbed it in. Then she took a pale yellow dress from the bedpost and began the struggle of getting Erin into it. "I hope Laura's going to church somewhere this morning."

Dylan thought back to the day when Laura's mother had driven away with her. Laura had waved to them out the back window until the car was out of sight. "Well, the caseworker in Tennessee said her mother goes pretty regularly."

"Poor thing. She took a lot of abuse from that husband of hers before she finally left." Susan had both of Erin's arms in the dress and was moving on toward the buttoning-up process. "Still . . . she left her only child."

"Don't be too hard on her," Dylan said, grinning down at his daughter's valiant struggle to remain unclothed. "Any woman might have under the circumstances."

"I suppose you're right." A cloud briefly crossed Susan's face. "Laura was only with us for three weeks and it seemed like we'd had her all her life."

"I know." Dylan turned the mobile, its wobbling, tinkling characters attracting Erin's attention and tempering her struggles against the dress. "Good news about Caleb. He goes before the pardon board in October of next year, and it's a cinch he'll make it with his good behavior."

"Really? When did you find out?"

"Yesterday afternoon. I wanted to save it as an Easter present for you."

"That's wonderful! I'm so glad for him."

"The chaplain told me Caleb's the best assistant he's ever had. And Jesse's already said he'd hire him at the cafe as soon as he makes parole."

Susan finished the buttons and began working the lacy socks on to Erin's peddling feet. "He'll have fun working with Jesse. What's he going to be doing?"

"To quote Jesse, Caleb's going to be the 'Assistant Chief Cook and Bottle Washer.' "

"Sounds impressive."

"I thought so." Dylan watched Christopher Robin and friends in their colorful, tinkling dance. "Billie LeBlanc's been writing to him in prison."

"I'm sure the judge is thrilled about that."

"Maybe not right now, but if Caleb turns out like I expect him to, the judge could change his mind."

Susan slipped the last shoe on and double-tied the knot.

"Now," she smiled, picking Erin up in her arms, "Her High-ness is ready to receive guests."

"Well, let's go, then. I'm sure they're waiting for her arrival before they start the service." Dylan looked at Susan, radiant in her pale green dress trimmed with lace at the collar and sleeves. "What a fortunate man I am."

"How so?"

"Should be obvious," Dylan said, nibbling Erin on her neck, turning over her giggle box again. "I'm escorting the two loveliest ladies in all of Evangeline."

"I can see you're astute as well," Susan said, heading for the hall. "Don't you think so, Erin?"

Erin gurgled and poked her thumb in her mouth by way of agreement.

Dylan opened the door and they stepped out onto the gal-lery. April sunshine, the color of fresh butter, shimmered on the wind-rippled water. "Couldn't ask for a better Easter morning."

Gazing at the green-gold cascade of the willow branches moving languidly in the soft breeze, Susan said, almost as though she were alone, "I wonder if the morning was this beautiful two thousand years ago."

Dylan put his arm around Susan's waist, and they walked down the steps and along the white path. Erin gazed about at the wonder of her first Easter morning, lifted her small voice in what could have passed as a song of celebration, then spit up on her mother's new dress.